The Weather Man

Terrell J. Brown

Dedication

To my mother, Rhonda Brown, my Uncle, Darryl Brown, and my Father, Stanley J. Gorrell, your unwavering support and guidance have been my rock. This book is dedicated to you for your impact and impartation in my life. And to every individual who has faced their storms and found it difficult to navigate alone, this book is for you. May it provide the help and guidance you need to manage the challenges ahead.

FORWARD

With the pen of a ready writer, my son Terrell J. Brown has crafted a profound guide that illuminates the path through life's tumultuous storms. In this book, readers will find not only wisdom but also a treasure trove of insights drawn from Terrell's own life experiences. His journey embodies resilience and strength, offering helpful tools for weathering life's inevitable challenges and emerging victorious. This book is a must-read for anyone who has faced situations that seemed insurmountable, those moments that made them feel as if they would never see the light at the end of the tunnel. Terrell's narrative is both relatable and inspiring, providing a roadmap to navigate the complexities of life. As you turn these pages, you will gain a deeper understanding of how to confront and overcome the obstacles that life presents. I encourage every reader to embrace this book as not just a source of inspiration but also as a practical guide. Terrell's experiences serve as a reminder that you are not alone in your struggles; many have walked this path and emerged stronger. His insights will empower you to take command of your journey, instilling hope and determination. This book comes highly recommended, not only for its engaging storytelling but also for its capacity to transform lives. May it serve as a beacon of light for those seeking guidance and reassurance in their own journeys.

- Dr. Stanley J. Gorrell

Terrell J. Brown

Table of Contents

About the Author

Terrell J. Brown, born on October 12, 1989, at St. John Hospital in Far Rockaway, is a multifaceted individual who wears many hats—a painter, philanthropist, and steadfast believer. His journey through life has been marked by resilience and determination, as he has faced and overcome a myriad of challenging storms, including bullying, grief, and the internal struggles that often accompany them. Growing up in Far Rockaway, New York, Terrell encountered his fair share of obstacles, each shaping his character and fueling his passion for self-expression and advocacy. Through art, he found an essential outlet to navigate these turbulent circumstances, allowing him to channel his experiences into creativity. In doing so, he discovered the power of finding his voice and charting a new path forward. Terrell understands that nothing in life can fully prepare us for the unexpected challenges we may face. Life often throws us curveballs that catch us off guard, but it is within these moments of adversity that we can find our strength. His journey is a testament to the belief that through struggle, we can emerge stronger and more compassionate, ready to uplift others in their battles. With a heart dedicated to giving back, Terrell continues to inspire those around him, using his art and philanthropy to make a positive impact on the world. He believes that regardless of the storms we face, there is always hope and the possibility of brighter days ahead.

Chapter 1:

The Developing Stage

In the journey of life, every individual will inevitably encounter challenges, difficulties, and periods of intense emotional and psychological upheaval—what we may aptly refer to as "life storms." These storms can manifest in various forms, such as the loss of a loved one, financial hardships, health crises, or relational conflicts. Just as natural storms are a part of the Earth's weather system, life storms are an intrinsic part of the human experience. They are unavoidable, often unpredictable, and can be both terrifying and transformative. However, like weather storms, they can be understood, prepared for, and managed.

The analogy between life storms and weather storms is both profound and instructive. In meteorology, storms develop due to specific atmospheric conditions—changes in temperature, pressure, and humidity—that create instability in the environment. Similarly, life storms arise from a confluence of personal circumstances, emotional states, and external factors that disrupt the equilibrium of our lives. Understanding the development of these storms is crucial for navigating through them with resilience and grace.

In this chapter, we will explore the foundational elements that contribute to the formation of life storms. We will delve into the significance of early life experiences in shaping our responses to future challenges, the interplay between nature and nurture, and the role of trauma in the development of personal storms. By examining these elements, we can gain insight into the root causes of our struggles and begin to cultivate the strength needed to weather them.

The earliest years of life, from birth to approximately five years of age, are a critical period in human development. During this time, the foundation for our emotional, psychological, and social well-being is laid. The experiences we have during these formative years profoundly influence how we perceive and respond to the world around us, particularly in times of difficulty.

In the same way that the early atmospheric conditions can determine the severity of a storm, our early life experiences can shape the intensity and nature of the storms we face later in life. The environment in which we are raised, the relationships we form with our caregivers, and the events we witness or endure during these years create the blueprint for our future emotional responses.

Children who grow up in stable, loving, and supportive environments are more likely to develop a sense of security and resilience. They learn that the world is a safe place, that their needs will be met, and that they are valued. These beliefs form the bedrock of their self-esteem and their ability to cope with challenges. On the other hand, children who experience neglect, abuse, or instability during these early years may develop a deep-seated sense of insecurity, mistrust, and fear. These early wounds can manifest as anxiety, depression, or other emotional difficulties later in life, making it harder to withstand life's inevitable storms.

The significance of early life experiences in shaping our

responses to adversity cannot be overstated. Just as a storm's path is influenced by the conditions present at its inception, our ability to navigate life's challenges is largely determined by the emotional and psychological groundwork laid in our early years.

The age-old debate of nature versus nurture is particularly relevant when examining the development of life storms. Are our responses to challenges predetermined by our genetic makeup, or are they shaped by the environment in which we are raised? The truth, as with many complex issues, lies somewhere in between.

Nature, or the genetic inheritance we receive from our parents, provides the raw material—the temperament, personality traits, and innate tendencies that influence how we perceive and interact with the world. Some individuals may be naturally more resilient, optimistic, or adaptable, while others may be more prone to anxiety, pessimism, or rigidity. These inherent traits form the foundation upon which our life experiences are built.

Nurture, on the other hand, refers to the environmental factors that influence our development, including our upbringing, relationships, education, and life experiences. These external factors can either reinforce or mitigate our natural tendencies. For example, a child with a naturally anxious temperament may learn to manage their anxiety effectively if raised in a supportive and understanding environment. Conversely, a child with a naturally resilient disposition may struggle if subjected to chronic stress or trauma.

The interplay between nature and nurture is dynamic and complex. While our genetic makeup provides a blueprint, it is our experiences—both positive and negative—that shape the structure of our emotional and psychological lives. This process occurs through both continuity and stages.

Continuity refers to the gradual development of emotional and psychological traits over time. For example, a child who is naturally cautious may become more cautious over time if their environment reinforces this trait. Stages, on the other hand, refer to distinct periods of development in which significant changes occur. These stages often correspond to major life transitions, such as starting school, entering adolescence, or becoming a parent. During these stages, individuals may experience profound shifts in their emotional and psychological makeup, often in response to the demands of their environment.

Stability and change are also key concepts in understanding the development of life storms. Stability refers to the enduring aspects of our personality and behavior that remain consistent over time. These stable traits provide a sense of continuity and identity, even in the face of change. However, change is also an inevitable part of life. Our experiences, relationships, and circumstances continuously shape and reshape who we are. The ability to adapt to change, to grow and evolve in response to life's challenges, is a crucial aspect of resilience.

Ultimately, the development of life storms is the result of a complex interplay between nature and nurture, continuity and stages, stability and change. By understanding these dynamics, we can begin to appreciate the factors that contribute to our struggles and take steps to manage them more effectively.

Trauma is a significant factor in the development of personal storms. Traumatic experiences—such as abuse, neglect, loss, or violence—can have a profound and lasting impact on an individual's emotional and psychological well-being. Trauma disrupts the normal process of development, creating deep wounds that can fester and grow over time, manifesting as anxiety, depression, or other emotional difficulties.

The effects of trauma can be particularly damaging when it occurs during the early years of life, a period when the brain is still developing, and the foundations of our emotional and psychological well-being are being laid. Early trauma can alter the brain's structure and function, leading to difficulties in regulating emotions, forming healthy relationships, and coping with stress. These changes can create a sense of vulnerability and insecurity that persists into adulthood, making it harder to navigate life's challenges.

However, trauma does not only occur in childhood. Traumatic experiences can happen at any stage of life, and their impact can be just as profound. Whether it's the sudden loss of a loved one, a serious illness, or an act of violence, trauma can shatter our sense of safety and stability, leaving us feeling overwhelmed and powerless.

The storms that result from trauma can be intense and long-lasting. They can affect every aspect of our lives, from our relationships to our careers to our sense of self. However, it is important to remember that trauma, while deeply painful, does not have to define us. With the right support and resources, it is possible to heal from trauma and develop the resilience needed to weather life's storms.

Healing from trauma often involves confronting the pain and fear that it has caused, which can be a difficult and frightening process. However, it is through this process of confrontation and healing that we can begin to reclaim our power and regain control over our lives. By facing our trauma head-on, we can learn to navigate the storms it has created and emerge stronger and more resilient on the other side.

Scripture: Psalm 32:7 (NLT) - "For you are my hiding place; you protect me from trouble. You surround me with songs of victory."

Let us turn to the wisdom of Scripture for comfort and guidance. Psalm 32:7 (NLT) reads: "For you are my hiding place; you protect me from trouble. You surround me with songs of victory." This verse serves as a powerful reminder that, even in the midst of life's storms, we are never alone. We have a refuge, a place of safety and protection, in the presence of God.

In the context of the storms of life, this verse offers both solace and strength. It assures us that, no matter how fierce the storm, there is always a place where we can find shelter. This hiding place is not an escape from our troubles but a space where we can gather our strength, find peace, and prepare to face the challenges ahead.

Moreover, the verse speaks of "songs of victory," a beautiful image that conveys the idea of triumph over adversity. These are not just songs of survival but of victory—celebrations of having overcome the storm and emerged stronger on the other side. It is a promise that, with faith and perseverance, we can not only survive our storms but also transform them into opportunities for growth and victory.

In times of trouble, it can be easy to feel overwhelmed to lose sight of the possibility of victory. But this verse encourages us to hold on to hope, to trust in the protection and guidance of a higher power, and to believe in the possibility of overcoming even the most daunting of challenges.

As we navigate the developing stage of life's storms, let us take comfort in the knowledge that we are not alone. We have the strength within us, shaped by our early experiences and refined by our challenges, to weather the storms that come our way. And we have the promise of victory, a reminder that no storm lasts forever and that, in the end, we can emerge stronger and more resilient than before.

The developing stage of life's storms is a complex and multifaceted process, shaped by a myriad of factors, including our early life experiences, the interplay between nature and nurture, and the impact of trauma. Understanding these factors can provide us with valuable insights into the root causes of our struggles and help us develop the resilience needed to navigate through them.

Life storms are an inevitable part of the human

experience. They are challenging, often painful, and can leave us feeling vulnerable and overwhelmed. However, they also offer us opportunities for growth, transformation, and victory. By understanding the development of these storms, we can learn to embrace them, to see them not as obstacles but as opportunities for growth and resilience.

As we continue on our journey through life, let us remember that we have the strength within us to weather any storm. Our early life experiences, our genetic makeup, and our ability to adapt and change all contribute to our resilience. And with faith, perseverance, and the support of those around us, we can overcome even the most challenging of storms.

In the chapters that follow, we will explore practical strategies for managing life's storms, drawing on both personal stories and timeless wisdom. We will learn how to find strength in adversity, how to navigate through difficult times with grace and resilience, and how to transform our challenges into opportunities for growth and victory. As we do so, let us keep in mind the words of Psalm 32:7, a reminder that, even in the darkest of times, we are surrounded by songs of victory and that with faith and perseverance, we can emerge stronger on the other side.

Chapter 2:

The Storm Conditions

In the vast expanse of human experience, storms are as unavoidable as the shifting seasons. These life storms—periods of profound emotional, psychological, and spiritual upheaval—are intrinsic to our journey. Just as meteorologists examine atmospheric conditions to predict and understand natural storms, so too must we delve into the environmental, emotional, and spiritual pressures that give rise to the storms within our lives. By recognizing and understanding these conditions, we equip ourselves to face them with wisdom and resilience.

Life's storms are not merely random disruptions; they are often the result of specific circumstances or pressures that build over time. These storms serve as both trials and opportunities for growth, forcing us to confront our deepest fears, weaknesses, and unresolved issues. In this chapter, we will explore six distinct types of life storms: **Self-Inflicted Storms, Internal Storms, Storms of Association or Agreement, Generational Storms, Divinely Caused Storms**, and **Warfare Storms**. Understanding these storms and the conditions that lead to their formation is crucial for navigating them effectively.

1. Self-Inflicted Storms

Self-inflicted storms arise from our own choices, often stemming from disobedience, poor decision-making, or a willful departure from the path of integrity and wisdom. These storms are the direct consequences of actions that go against our better judgment or moral principles. When we ignore the inner voice of guidance, whether it be our conscience, spiritual intuition, or ethical reasoning, we often find ourselves in turbulent situations of our own making.

The story of Jonah serves as a timeless example of a self-inflicted storm. Jonah's decision to flee from God's command led him into a literal storm, symbolizing the inner turmoil and external consequences that follow disobedience. His plight illustrates how our actions not only affect us but also have repercussions for those around us. The storms we create through our choices are not just about us—they often impact our relationships, our environment, and our future.

- **Recognizing the Root Causes**: Self-inflicted storms are often the result of deep-seated fears, unhealed wounds, or unresolved internal conflicts. To navigate out of these storms, we must first acknowledge the underlying issues that drive our actions. "Recognizing the root of your pattern is the only way to eradicate it from your life." This introspection is crucial; it requires us to be honest with ourselves, and to confront the uncomfortable truths about why we make the choices we do. By understanding these roots, we can begin to alter our patterns and make decisions that align with our true values.

- **The Role of Free Will**: Free will is both a gift and a responsibility. It allows us to shape our destiny, but it also holds us accountable for the consequences of our actions. The paradox of free will is that while it empowers us to make choices, it also binds us to the outcomes of those choices. When we misuse this power—by acting impulsively, selfishly, or without regard for the consequences—we set in motion forces that lead to self-inflicted storms. However, the same free will that leads us into these storms can also lead us out. By choosing differently and aligning our actions with wisdom and integrity, we can change the course of our lives.

- **Separating Actions from Identity**: It is essential to understand that our actions, while significant, do not define our identity. The storms we create through poor decisions are not reflections of who we are at our core; rather, they are the results of specific choices made in specific circumstances. By separating our actions from our identity, we free ourselves from the burden of guilt and shame, allowing room for growth and transformation. Our identity is fluid, shaped by the lessons we learn and the changes we make in response to life's storms.

2. Internal Storms

Internal storms are those that rage within us, often triggered by trauma, heartbreak, or unresolved emotional pain. These storms manifest as deep inner turmoil—feelings of anxiety, depression, fear, or despair that churn within our minds and hearts. Unlike external storms, which are visible and tangible, internal storms are often hidden from view, making them all the more insidious and difficult to navigate.

These storms can be sparked by a variety of factors: the loss of a loved one, the end of a significant relationship, a profound personal failure, or the resurfacing of past traumas. They represent the internal conflicts and emotional wounds that we carry, often unresolved and unhealed. Internal storms can leave us feeling lost, adrift, and overwhelmed by the intensity of our own emotions.

- **The Hidden Battles**: Internal storms are akin to the quiet yet powerful undercurrents in the ocean. They may not always be visible on the surface, but they have the power to pull us under to erode our sense of self and stability. These storms challenge us to confront the darker aspects of our psyche—the fears, doubts, and insecurities that we often try to bury. Yet, in facing these internal storms, we also find the opportunity for profound healing and personal growth.

- **Healing from Within**: The process of healing internal storms requires deep introspection and a willingness to confront the pain that lies within. This healing journey is often non-linear, involving cycles of reflection, acceptance, and release. Engaging in practices such as therapy, meditation, journaling, or spiritual counseling can help us navigate these storms. By acknowledging our emotions and giving ourselves permission to feel and process them, we begin to calm the storm within and restore our inner peace.

- **Hope as a Lifeline**: In the midst of internal storms, hope becomes our lifeline. The belief that there is a way through the darkness, that healing and renewal are possible, is what sustains us in the most challenging moments. Hope is not just a passive wish; it is an active choice to hold on, to keep moving forward, even when the path ahead is unclear. This hope anchors us, providing the stability needed to weather the storm and emerge stronger on the other side.

- **Transforming Suffering into Wisdom**: Internal storms, while painful, offer the potential for deep transformation. Suffering can be a catalyst for growth, a crucible in which our pain is transformed into wisdom, compassion, and resilience. The ancient concept of the "dark night of the soul" speaks to this process—a period of intense inner struggle that precedes spiritual awakening. By embracing the challenges of our internal storms, we allow them to shape us into wiser, more compassionate beings capable of navigating life's challenges with greater grace and understanding.

3. Storms of Association or Agreement

Storms of association or agreement arise from the company we keep and the environments in which we immerse ourselves. These storms are not solely of our own making, but they result from the influence of others— whether through relationships, social circles, or the broader societal context. The values, behaviors, and attitudes of those we associate with can significantly impact our lives, sometimes leading us into storms that we never anticipated.

It is often said that "we are the sum of the five people we spend the most time with." This adage underscores the profound influence that our associations have on us. When we align ourselves with individuals or groups whose values, behaviors, or attitudes conflict with our own, we expose ourselves to potential storms of conflict, confusion, and inner turmoil. These storms can manifest as relational discord, ethical dilemmas, or crises of identity as we struggle to reconcile the dissonance between who we are and the influences we have allowed into our lives.

• **The Influence of Environment**: The environments we engage with—whether in our personal relationships, professional settings, or social circles—play a crucial role in shaping our thoughts, beliefs, and actions. Just as a drop of dye colors an entire glass of water, the influence of others can subtly but powerfully color our perceptions and decisions. This is why it is essential to choose our associations with care, ensuring that we surround ourselves with individuals and environments that uplift, support, and align with our core values.

- **Choosing Associations Wisely**: The key to avoiding storms of association lies in discernment. We must be vigilant about the energy and values we allow into our lives, recognizing that not all relationships are beneficial, and some may even be harmful. This discernment involves setting boundaries, saying no to toxic influences, and seeking out relationships that are based on mutual respect, understanding, and shared principles. It also means being willing to walk away from relationships or environments that no longer serve our growth, even if it is difficult to do so.

- **The Courage to Disassociate**: Disassociating from negative influences requires courage and clarity of purpose. It means standing firm in our values, even when it is uncomfortable or when others do not understand our choices. It also involves being honest with ourselves about the impact that certain people or environments are having on our well-being. By doing so, we protect our inner peace and create space for healthier, more positive relationships and environments to enter our lives.

- **The Ripple Effect of Positive Associations**: Just as negative associations can lead to storms, positive associations can create a ripple effect of growth, healing, and transformation. When we surround ourselves with people who encourage us to reach our highest potential, we are more likely to make decisions that align with our true values and purpose. This positive influence extends beyond ourselves, impacting those around us and contributing to a collective upliftment. In this way, choosing our associations wisely is not just an act of self-preservation but a contribution to the greater good.

4. Generational Storms

Generational storms are those passed down through family lines—patterns of behavior, belief systems, or emotional baggage inherited from previous generations. These storms are deeply rooted in the past, involving long-standing issues such as inherited trauma, familial conflicts, or entrenched habits and mindsets that have been passed down unconsciously.

The concept of generational storms speaks to the notion that we are not isolated individuals but part of a continuum, a lineage that stretches back through time. We inherit not only physical traits but also emotional and psychological patterns from our ancestors. These inherited storms can manifest in our lives as recurring patterns of behavior, such as cycles of addiction, abuse, or chronic emotional issues, that seem to repeat across generations.

- **The Weight of Inheritance**: The weight of inheritance can be both a burden and a blessing. On the one hand, we may find ourselves grappling with issues that are not entirely our own but are part of our family's legacy. On the other hand, this awareness gives us the opportunity to break the cycle, heal the wounds of the past, and create a new legacy for future generations.

- **Breaking the Cycle**: Breaking free from generational storms requires a deliberate and often challenging effort. It involves recognizing the patterns that have been passed down to us and making a conscious decision to live differently. This might involve seeking therapy to address inherited trauma, exploring our family history to understand the roots of certain behaviors, or simply resolving to break free from the destructive cycles that have plagued our lineage. Breaking the cycle is not just an act of self-healing; it is an act of liberation that frees future generations from the burdens of the past.

- **The Courage to Confront the Past**: Confronting the past is no easy task. It requires us to face the shadow side of our family history, to acknowledge the pain and dysfunction that has been passed down, and to take responsibility for our own healing. This process can be painful, but it is also empowering. By choosing to confront and heal these generational wounds, we reclaim our power and create the possibility of a different future.

- **Legacy of Change**: When we confront and overcome generational storms, we do more than just heal ourselves—we change the course of our family history. We become the point at which the old patterns stop, and new possibilities begin. By addressing these deep-rooted issues, we set a new precedent for those who follow, creating a legacy of strength, resilience, and positive transformation. This is the ultimate act of generational healing: to turn the storms of the past into a legacy of hope for the future.

5. Divinely Caused Storms

Divinely caused storms are those orchestrated by a higher power for purposes that often go beyond our immediate understanding. These storms might be intended to test our obedience, protect us from unseen dangers, or purify us through challenging experiences. While these storms can be difficult to endure, they often serve a greater purpose in our spiritual growth.

The story of Job is a powerful example of a divinely caused storm. Despite his righteousness, Job faced immense suffering, not as a punishment but as a test of his faith and resilience. Through his trials, Job's character was refined, and his faith deepened, illustrating that even the most severe storms can lead to profound spiritual growth.

- **Obedience and Trust**: Obedience storms occur when we follow a path that we believe is divinely ordained yet find ourselves in the midst of great trials. These storms test our faith and commitment, reminding us that if we are led into a storm, the same power that led us in can also lead us out. Trusting in divine guidance during these times is essential.

- **Purification Through Trials**: Purification storms are those that strip away the impurities in our lives, whether they be toxic relationships, destructive habits, or limiting beliefs. These storms are not meant to destroy us but to refine us, much like gold is refined in fire. Through these trials, we emerge stronger and more aligned with our true purpose.

- **Protection in Disguise**: Some storms come as a form of protection. What appears to be a setback or a hardship may actually be a divine intervention, removing us from harmful situations or preventing greater disasters. In hindsight, these protection storms reveal their true purpose, reminding us that not all disruptions are harmful; some are necessary for our well-being.

6. Warfare Storms

Warfare storms are intense battles that occur in the spiritual or emotional realms, often manifesting in our physical lives. These storms are the result of conflicts between opposing forces—light and darkness, good and evil—and they challenge us to stand firm in our beliefs and values.

Warfare storms are not just about survival; they are about victory. They require us to engage in spiritual warfare, using the tools of faith, prayer, and perseverance to overcome the forces that seek to derail our progress. These storms test our resolve and demand deep inner strength, but they also offer the opportunity for significant spiritual growth.

- **Equipped for Battle**: In the face of warfare storms, it is crucial to remember that we are not left defenseless. We have been given spiritual weapons—faith, prayer, wisdom—to fight these battles. By recognizing the spiritual nature of these storms, we can approach them with the right mindset and strategies, ensuring that we not only survive but emerge victorious.

- **Victory Through Faith**: Warfare storms challenge our faith, but they also offer the potential for great spiritual victories. By standing firm in our beliefs and relying on divine strength, we can overcome even the most daunting of these storms. The battles we face in warfare storms are not just about the present moment; they shape our spiritual journey and prepare us for future challenges.

Just as natural storms play a vital role in the Earth's ecosystem, life's storms serve a purpose in our personal and spiritual growth. Understanding the unique conditions that lead to these storms allows us to recognize the early warning signs and triggers, giving us the opportunity to prepare and respond effectively. By doing so, we transform these storms from sources of suffering into opportunities for growth and resilience.

Psalm 40:1-3 (ESV) provides a profound source of comfort and guidance in the midst of life's storms:

"I waited patiently for the Lord; he inclined to me and heard my cry. He drew me up from the pit of destruction, out of the miry bog, and set my feet upon a rock, making my steps secure."

This passage encapsulates the journey through a storm—from the depths of despair to the stability and security that come from divine intervention and guidance. It reminds us that patience and faith are essential when navigating life's storms. Even in the darkest moments, when we feel trapped in the "miry bog" of our circumstances, there is always the possibility of being lifted up, of finding solid ground once again.

- **Waiting Patiently for the Lord**: The act of waiting patiently is not passive; it requires strength, resilience, and a deep trust in the process of life. When faced with storms, our instinct may be to resist, to fight against the forces that seem to be tearing our lives apart. But sometimes, the most powerful response is to wait, to trust that the storm will pass and that we will emerge from it stronger and more secure. In this waiting, we are not alone—God hears our cries, and in His time, He draws us out of the pit of destruction.

- **The Pit of Destruction and the Miry Bog**: These metaphors powerfully describe the feelings of being overwhelmed, stuck, and helpless in the face of life's storms. The "pit of destruction" represents the deepest, darkest places we can find ourselves—whether through self-inflicted storms, the legacy of generational storms, or the intense battles of warfare storms. The "miry bog" symbolizes the confusion and entanglement that often accompany these storms, where every step seems to sink us deeper into despair. Yet, even here, the promise of divine intervention gives us hope.

- **Set Upon a Rock, Steps Made Secure**: The imagery of being set upon a rock speaks to the restoration of stability and strength. After the storm has passed, after we have been drawn out of the pit, there is a return to solid ground—a place where we can once again stand firm. This rock symbolizes the unshakeable foundation that comes from faith, wisdom, and the lessons learned through the storm. Our steps, once unsure and faltering, are now made secure, guided by the clarity and understanding gained from enduring the storm.

- **The Transformation of Storms into Growth**: Ultimately, the storms of life are transformative. They strip away the illusions, the superficialities, and the distractions, revealing what is truly essential. They force us to confront our vulnerabilities, our fears, and our weaknesses, but they also reveal our strengths, our resilience, and our capacity for growth. By understanding the unique conditions that lead to these storms, we can approach them not as threats, but as opportunities for deeper self-awareness and spiritual maturation.

As we journey through life, storms will come—some of our own making, some inherited, and some orchestrated by forces beyond our understanding. Each type of storm presents its own challenges, but each also offers the potential for profound growth and transformation. By understanding the conditions that lead to these storms, recognizing the early warning signs, and grounding ourselves in faith, we can navigate these turbulent times with greater wisdom and grace.

Psalm 40:1-3 reminds us that no storm is permanent. There is always a way out, a path to solid ground. And while the journey through the storm may be difficult, it is also a journey toward greater strength, clarity, and purpose. By embracing the storms we face, we open ourselves to the possibility of not just surviving, but thriving—emerging from the tempest not just intact, but transformed, with our feet set upon a rock and our steps made secure.

In the end, life's storms are not just disruptions—they are divine opportunities for growth, purification, and the deepening of our faith. By facing these storms with courage, patience, and trust in the process, we can transform them into the very forces that propel us toward our true potential.

Chapter 3:

Instability in the Atmosphere

Life, like the atmosphere surrounding our planet, is a delicate equilibrium of forces. These forces, invisible yet powerful, include our thoughts, emotions, and experiences. They are the unseen currents that shape the weather within our souls, creating a landscape constantly in flux. When these internal and external forces fall out of balance, they create instability—the precursor to the storms that can shake the very foundation of our existence.

This chapter delves into the essence of this instability, examining how internal motivations, subconscious influences, negative thoughts, and self-doubt intertwine with external pressures from relationships, environments, and societal expectations. We will explore how these factors collectively create turbulence in our lives, leading us into the heart of life's storms. Through this exploration, we can begin to understand how to find stability amid chaos, and, ultimately, how to weather these storms with grace and resilience.

At the core of our being lies the subconscious, a vast and complex realm where our deepest motivations, fears, and desires reside. This hidden part of ourselves is like the deep ocean—dark, mysterious, and filled with powerful currents that we often cannot see or control. Yet, these currents have a profound impact on the surface of our lives, influencing our thoughts, behaviors, and emotional responses in ways we may not even be aware of.

The subconscious mind is a repository of all our past experiences, beliefs, and emotional memories. From the moment we are born, every experience we have, every interaction, and every emotion, is stored away in this vast internal database. Over time, these experiences form patterns—ways of thinking and behaving that become automatic, guiding our actions and reactions without our conscious awareness.

These patterns can be beneficial, providing us with a sense of stability and predictability in our lives. However, they can also be detrimental, particularly when they are rooted in negative or traumatic experiences. For instance, a person who has experienced rejection or abandonment in their early life may develop a deep-seated fear of being alone. This fear, although buried deep within the subconscious, can manifest in a variety of ways—clinging to unhealthy relationships, avoiding intimacy, or even sabotaging potential connections out of fear of rejection.

This is the essence of internal instability: when our subconscious motivations and fears are out of alignment with our conscious goals and desires, we experience a dissonance that creates internal turbulence. This turbulence, if left unchecked, can give rise to the storms of life— emotional upheaval, psychological distress, and behavioral patterns that perpetuate our suffering.

The journey to stability, therefore, begins with self-awareness. We must be willing to dive into the depths of our subconscious, to explore the patterns that have shaped our lives, and to confront the fears and desires that drive our actions. This process requires courage, honesty, and a willingness to face the darker aspects of our psyche. It involves asking ourselves difficult questions: What drives my actions? What am I truly afraid of? What do I desire most deeply, and why?

In exploring these questions, we begin to unravel the complex web of our internal motivations. We start to see how our past experiences have shaped our present behavior, and we gain insight into the patterns that may be holding us back. This understanding is the first step toward achieving emotional stability and preventing the internal unrest that can lead to life's storms.

However, understanding alone is not enough. We must also take action to realign our internal world with our conscious goals and values. This may involve challenging long-held beliefs, confronting unresolved emotions, or even changing our behavior in ways that feel uncomfortable or unfamiliar. But by doing so, we create a foundation of stability within ourselves—a foundation that can withstand the storms of life.

Just as a storm in the atmosphere begins with the formation of dark clouds, the storms within us often begin with the gathering of negative thoughts. These thoughts, like ominous clouds on the horizon, can overshadow our lives, casting a shadow of doubt and despair that can be difficult to escape.

Negative thoughts are not merely fleeting ideas; they are powerful forces that can shape our reality. They often arise from distorted thinking patterns—ways of perceiving the world that are colored by past experiences, fears, and insecurities. These patterns can lead us to interpret events in ways that reinforce our negative beliefs about ourselves and the world around us.

For example, a person who struggles with low self-esteem may interpret a minor setback at work as a confirmation of their inadequacy. This thought, in turn, triggers a cascade of negative emotions—anxiety, shame, and self-doubt—that can spiral out of control, leading to a full-blown emotional storm.

Self-doubt, in particular, is a potent source of internal instability. It undermines our confidence, making us question our abilities, our decisions, and our worth. When we doubt ourselves, we become hesitant and fearful, second-guessing our choices and avoiding risks. This hesitation creates instability, as we are no longer grounded in our sense of self or our ability to navigate life's challenges.

The impact of negative thoughts and self-doubt can be profound. They can erode our sense of self-worth, leading to feelings of hopelessness and despair. They can also create a cycle of self-sabotage, where our fear of failure or rejection causes us to avoid opportunities for growth and success. Over time, this cycle can become a self-fulfilling prophecy, trapping us in a storm of our own making.

To break free from this cycle, we must learn to challenge our negative thoughts and replace them with more positive and realistic perspectives. This involves recognizing that our thoughts are not facts—they are simply interpretations of reality, shaped by our past experiences and current mindset. By questioning the validity of our negative thoughts, we can begin to shift our perspective and open ourselves up to new possibilities.

One effective way to challenge negative thoughts is through the practice of cognitive restructuring. This involves identifying the negative thoughts that trigger our emotional distress and replacing them with more balanced and constructive thoughts. For example, instead of thinking, "I'm a failure because I made a mistake," we can reframe the thought as, "Everyone makes mistakes; this is an opportunity to learn and grow."

Another powerful tool for combating negative thoughts is the practice of mindfulness. By cultivating awareness of our thoughts and emotions in the present moment, we can observe them without judgment and without becoming entangled in them. This allows us to create space between our thoughts and our reactions, giving us the opportunity to choose how we respond.

Ultimately, overcoming negative thoughts and self-doubt requires a combination of self-awareness, cognitive strategies, and a commitment to self-compassion. It involves recognizing our inherent worth and believing in our ability to navigate life's challenges. As Psalm 55:22 (NIV) reminds us, "Cast your cares on the Lord, and he will sustain you; he will never let the righteous be shaken." This verse offers a powerful reminder that we are not alone in our struggles, and that by placing our trust in a higher power, we can find the strength and stability to weather the storms of life.

While much of the instability we experience originates within us, external influences also play a significant role in shaping our internal world. Relationships, environments, and societal pressures can all contribute to the turbulence we feel, either exacerbating existing instability or creating new sources of unrest.

Relationships, in particular, have a profound impact on our emotional and psychological well-being. The people we surround ourselves with can either uplift us or drag us down, depending on the nature of the relationship. In this sense, our connections with others can be seen as either stabilizing or destabilizing forces in our lives.

Toxic relationships—those characterized by manipulation, control, or constant conflict—create a sense of instability, making us feel insecure, anxious, and ungrounded. These relationships are like storms in their own right, creating emotional turmoil that can overshadow all other aspects of our lives. They sap our energy, erode our self-esteem, and leave us feeling emotionally drained.

On the other hand, supportive and nurturing relationships provide a stabilizing force, offering comfort, reassurance, and a sense of belonging. These relationships act as safe harbors, providing us with a sense of security and grounding that helps us navigate the storms of life. They remind us that we are not alone, that we are valued, and that we have a network of support to rely on.

The environment we live and work in also plays a crucial role in our emotional state. A chaotic or stressful environment can trigger feelings of anxiety and overwhelm, while a calm and organized space can promote a sense of peace and stability. The physical surroundings, social dynamics, and even the cultural context we inhabit all contribute to the overall atmosphere in which we live. When these external factors are negative or misaligned with our values, they can create a sense of dissonance and instability.

For example, living in a noisy, cluttered, or chaotic environment can make it difficult to find peace and clarity. Similarly, working in a toxic or high-pressure work environment can lead to chronic stress and burnout, further contributing to our internal instability. In contrast, creating a home or workspace that is organized, calm, and aligned with our values can help to foster a sense of stability and well-being.

Societal pressures further compound this instability. The expectations and demands placed on us by society—whether in terms of success, appearance, or behavior—can create a constant undercurrent of stress and dissatisfaction. The pressure to conform, to meet certain standards, or to achieve specific milestones can lead to feelings of inadequacy and self-doubt, further destabilizing our internal world.

These external influences are like winds that can either steady or destabilize our internal atmosphere. Just as a ship must adjust its sails to navigate the changing winds, we must be mindful of the external influences in our lives and how they affect our internal state. This involves being selective about the relationships we invest in, creating environments that support our well-being, and critically examining the societal expectations we choose to internalize.

To mitigate the impact of these external influences, it is

essential to cultivate a strong sense of self and to establish healthy boundaries. This means being discerning about the people and environments we allow into our lives, and taking steps to protect our emotional and psychological well-being. It also involves being mindful of the societal pressures we internalize, and recognizing that we have the power to define our own values and standards.

By taking control of these external influences, we can reduce the instability they create and foster a more balanced and grounded life. This, in turn, helps us to navigate the inevitable storms of life with greater resilience and equanimity.

Instability, whether internal or external, creates the perfect conditions for life's storms to develop. When we are emotionally or psychologically unbalanced, we become more susceptible to the triggers and stressors that can escalate into full-blown crises. Just as unstable air in the atmosphere can lead to the formation of thunderstorms, instability in our lives creates the conditions for emotional and psychological turbulence.

This turbulence often manifests as feelings of overwhelm, confusion, and anxiety. We may find ourselves caught in a cycle of negative thinking, unable to make decisions or take action. Our relationships may suffer as we become more reactive, defensive, or withdrawn. We may feel a sense of disconnect from ourselves and our purpose, leading to a loss of direction and meaning in life.

The process by which instability leads to turbulence is often gradual. It begins with small disruptions—negative thoughts, unresolved emotions, or external pressures—that go unnoticed or unaddressed. Over time, these small disruptions accumulate, creating a growing sense of unease and discomfort. If left unchecked, this instability can escalate, leading to more severe emotional and psychological disturbances, such as anxiety, depression, or even a full-blown crisis.

Turbulence in life is not merely the result of external events; it is the culmination of internal and external factors that have been left unresolved. When we fail to address the sources of instability in our lives, we create a fertile ground for turbulence to take hold. This turbulence can manifest in a variety of ways—through emotional outbursts, conflicts in relationships, or a sense of aimlessness and despair.

One of the key factors in preventing instability from leading to turbulence is self-awareness. By recognizing the early warning signs of instability—such as negative thought patterns, unresolved emotions, or external pressures—we can take proactive steps to address them before they escalate into a full-blown storm.

This might involve seeking support from a therapist or counselor, practicing mindfulness or meditation, or making changes in our relationships or environment. It might also involve developing new coping strategies, such as journaling, exercise, or creative expression, to help us manage stress and maintain our emotional and psychological balance.

Ultimately, the key to navigating turbulence in life is to develop a strong sense of self and cultivate resilience. This means being grounded in our values and beliefs, having a clear sense of purpose, and being able to adapt to changing circumstances with grace and flexibility. It also means being willing to confront the sources of instability in our lives and take action to address them before they escalate into a storm.

In times of instability, we can find comfort and guidance in the words of Scripture. Psalm 55:22 (NIV) offers a powerful message of reassurance: "Cast your cares on the Lord, and he will sustain you; he will never let the righteous be shaken." This verse reminds us that we are not alone in our struggles and that we have a source of strength and stability that we can rely on.

The act of casting our cares on the Lord is an act of trust and surrender. It involves acknowledging that we cannot control everything and that it is okay to seek help and support. By placing our faith in a higher power, we can find the strength to face our challenges with confidence, knowing that we are supported and sustained.

This verse also speaks to the idea of resilience. The promise that "he will never let the righteous be shaken" suggests that, no matter how turbulent our lives may become, we can remain grounded and stable in our faith. This stability is not about being unaffected by life's challenges but about having the inner strength and resilience to withstand them.

In the context of life's storms, Psalm 55:22 serves as a reminder that instability does not have to lead to turmoil. By placing our trust in the Lord and relying on our faith, we can navigate the challenges we face with grace and resilience, knowing that we are supported every step of the way.

This verse also invites us to let go of the burdens that weigh us down. It encourages us to release our worries, fears, and doubts, and to trust that we are not alone in our journey. By doing so, we free ourselves from the emotional and psychological instability that can lead to turbulence, and we create space for peace, clarity, and stability to enter our lives.

Instability is an inevitable part of life, but it does not have to define us. By understanding the internal and external factors that contribute to our instability, we can take proactive steps to create a more balanced and grounded life. This involves bringing subconscious influences into awareness, challenging negative thoughts and self-doubt, and managing the external pressures that impact our emotional and psychological well-being.

As we navigate the storms of life, let us remember the wisdom of Psalm 55:22. By casting our cares on the Lord and trusting in His sustenance, we can find the strength and stability we need to weather any storm. With faith, resilience, and a commitment to personal growth, we can turn instability into an opportunity for transformation, emerging stronger and more grounded on the other side.

This journey is not easy, nor is it linear. It requires a deep commitment to self-awareness, growth, and healing. It demands that we confront the sources of instability in our lives, whether they originate within us or in the external world. But it also offers the promise of profound transformation—a transformation that allows us to move through life with greater ease, clarity, and purpose.

In the end, the storms of life are not to be feared but embraced. They are opportunities for growth, for deepening our understanding of ourselves, and for strengthening our faith. By embracing stability in a turbulent world, we can navigate these storms with grace, resilience, and a sense of inner peace, knowing that we are supported by a force greater than ourselves.

Chapter 4:

Something that Triggered Motion

This chapter explores the catalysts that set life's storms into motion. These catalysts, whether they manifest as sudden, dramatic events or as subtle, gradual developments, have the power to disrupt the equilibrium of our lives. Through a philosophical and metaphysical lens, we will examine the nature of these triggers, how they intersect with our personal choices and external circumstances, and the profound impact they have on our spiritual and emotional journey. This exploration will also delve into the concept of cumulative effects, where minor, seemingly inconsequential events combine to precipitate significant upheaval, and will draw upon the wisdom of Psalm 46:1-3 to offer comfort and guidance in the midst of these life-altering experiences.

Life, in all its complexity, is a dynamic interplay of forces, both visible and hidden. We move through our days often unaware of the delicate balance that holds our existence together—until something, a sudden flash of lightning or a slow, gathering storm, disrupts that balance. These moments, these triggers, are the catalysts that set our internal and external worlds into motion, sometimes with the force of a hurricane, other times with the persistent, relentless push of a rising tide. They are the moments when the still waters of our lives are stirred, bringing to the surface emotions, memories, and fears that have long lain dormant.

At the heart of every storm, there lies a trigger—a singular event or a combination of circumstances that ignites the tempest. These triggers are as varied as the human experience itself. Some arrive suddenly, like a bolt of lightning that splits the sky, leaving us in shock, reeling from the impact. Others approach more slowly, like a distant thunderhead that gradually darkens the horizon, giving us time to watch, to worry, and to brace ourselves for the inevitable.

Consider, for a moment, the unexpected loss of a loved one. Such a loss can feel like a seismic shift in our reality, a rupture in the fabric of our existence that leaves us disoriented and struggling to find solid ground. The grief that follows is a storm unto itself—an emotional maelstrom that sweeps through our lives, upending our sense of normalcy, challenging our beliefs, and forcing us to confront the fragility of life. In this storm, we may find ourselves questioning everything: the meaning of life, the nature of death, and the purpose of our own journey.

Similarly, the experience of betrayal can serve as a powerful trigger. When someone we trust deceives us, it is as if the very ground beneath our feet has been pulled away, leaving us to freefall into a void of uncertainty. The storm of betrayal is one of disillusionment and despair, a tumultuous blend of anger, sadness, and confusion. It forces us to reassess our relationships, our boundaries, and the way we navigate the world. This storm can be especially fierce because it strikes at the core of our need for connection and trust, shaking the foundations of our emotional security.

Yet, not all triggers are immediate or dramatic. Some are subtle, creeping into our lives over time. Imagine the slow accumulation of stress in a demanding job. Day by day, the pressure builds—a missed deadline here, a critical performance review there. Each small stressor may seem insignificant on its own, but together, they create a perfect storm. One day, a minor issue—a snide remark from a colleague, perhaps—becomes the final straw, unleashing a torrent of frustration, exhaustion, and burnout. The storm that follows may manifest as a sudden outburst, a decision to quit, or a breakdown in mental and emotional health.

These examples illustrate how triggers, whether sudden or gradual, are integral to the formation of life's storms. They are the sparks that ignite our unspoken fears, unresolved conflicts, and unmet needs. But what is it about these events or circumstances that give them such power? Why do they have the ability to throw our lives into disarray?

Our lives are shaped by the choices we make, each decision a thread in the intricate tapestry of our existence. Some of these decisions are minor, barely registering in our consciousness, while others are monumental, marking pivotal moments in our journey. Yet, every decision, no matter how small, carries within it the potential to set off a chain reaction of events that can lead to unforeseen consequences.

When we consider the role of personal decisions in triggering life's storms, we enter a realm where free will meets fate, where our autonomy intersects with the larger forces of the universe. It is in our decisions that we exercise our power, for better or worse, and it is through our actions that we shape our destiny.

Take, for example, the decision to pursue a particular

career path. On the surface, this choice may seem straightforward—motivated by passion, opportunity, or necessity. But as we delve deeper into this path, we encounter a series of challenges: the pressure to succeed, the demands of the job, and the sacrifices required. Each of these challenges adds weight to the burden we carry, and if we are not careful, this burden can become overwhelming. The storm that results—whether it manifests as burnout, disillusionment, or a mid-life crisis—forces us to confront the consequences of our choices. It asks us to reevaluate our priorities, our values, and our true desires.

Similarly, consider the decision to enter into a relationship. This choice, filled with hope and expectation, can lead to deep emotional fulfillment. However, relationships are also fraught with challenges—miscommunications, unmet expectations, and the inevitable conflicts that arise from two people trying to merge their lives. Over time, these challenges can accumulate, creating a storm of emotional turbulence. If not addressed, this turbulence can escalate, leading to a breakdown in the relationship, heartache, and the need to start anew.

In both examples, the storms that arise from our decisions serve as reminders of the complexity of human life. They teach us that our actions have consequences, and that our free will, while a gift, is also a responsibility. You can choose your decisions, but you can choose the consequences. The storms we create through our choices are not punishments but opportunities for growth. They challenge us to learn from our mistakes, to make more informed decisions, and to approach life with greater wisdom and humility.

While personal decisions play a significant role in triggering life's storms, we must also acknowledge the impact of external events—forces that lie beyond our control. These events are like natural disasters: sudden, often unpredictable, and capable of causing widespread devastation. They remind us of the fragility of life, of the thin veneer of stability that can be shattered in an instant.

Consider the sudden loss of a job. For many, employment is more than just a means of income; it is a source of identity, purpose, and security. When that job is lost—whether due to economic downturns, company restructuring, or other unforeseen circumstances—the impact can be profound. The storm that follows is one of uncertainty, fear, and anxiety. It forces us to confront the reality of our situation, to reassess our skills and value in the job market, and to find a new path forward.

Another powerful external trigger is the onset of illness, particularly when it strikes without warning. Health is something we often take for granted, assuming that our bodies will continue to function as they always have. But when illness strikes, it disrupts our lives in ways we cannot always anticipate. The storm of illness is both physical and emotional, as we grapple with pain, limitation, and the fear of what lies ahead. It challenges our resilience, our faith, and our ability to adapt to new realities.

The ending of a significant relationship is yet another external event that can trigger a life storm. Whether through divorce, separation, or the death of a loved one, such endings are seismic shifts that alter the landscape of our lives. The storm that follows is a complex blend of grief, loss, and the need to rebuild. It is a time of profound vulnerability, where the future feels uncertain, and the past haunts us with memories and regrets.

In each of these cases, the storms are not of our own making, yet they demand our response. They force us to adapt, to find new sources of strength, and to rebuild our lives on a different foundation. These external triggers remind us that while we may not be able to control the events that come our way, we can control how we respond to them. They challenge us to find resilience in the face of adversity, to seek meaning in our suffering, and to trust in the process of life, even when it leads us through the darkest of storms.

While some storms are triggered by singular, dramatic events, others are the result of a slow, steady build-up of pressure—what is often referred to as "the last straw." These storms are the culmination of many smaller, seemingly insignificant factors that, over time, create a situation that is ripe for disruption. The final trigger, the "last straw," may appear trivial in isolation, but it is the point at which the accumulated pressure can no longer be contained, and the storm breaks with full force.

The concept of "the last straw" is a powerful reminder of the cumulative effects of stress, frustration, and unresolved issues. It teaches us that storms are not always sudden or unexpected; often, they are the result of a gradual process, one that we may not even be fully aware of until it reaches its breaking point.

Consider the experience of a person who has been quietly struggling with the demands of life—juggling work, family responsibilities, and personal challenges. Each day, they push through, managing to keep everything together, but just barely. Over time, the weight of these responsibilities begins to take its toll. They may feel increasingly tired, irritable, and disconnected from their own needs and desires. Then, one day, something small happens—perhaps they spill coffee on their favorite shirt, or they receive a minor criticism at work—and suddenly, everything falls apart. The storm that ensues is not really about the spilled coffee or the criticism; it is about the accumulation of stress that has been building up for months, even years.

This type of storm, triggered by the "last straw," serves as a wake-up call. It forces us to acknowledge the pressures and stresses we have been ignoring or downplaying. It challenges us to take a step back, to reassess our lives, and to make the changes necessary to restore balance and well-being. These storms are often the most transformative, as they reveal the deeper issues that have been festering beneath the surface, issues that we can no longer afford to ignore.

In some cases, the cumulative effects that lead to a storm are not just personal but systemic. For example, consider a community that has been dealing with economic hardship, social injustice, and environmental degradation for many years. Each of these issues may be manageable on its own, but together, they create a volatile situation. The "last straw" might be a specific event—a police shooting, a natural disaster, or a political decision—that triggers a collective storm of protest, unrest, or even revolution. In this context, the storm is not just a personal experience but a societal one, reflecting the accumulated frustrations and grievances of an entire community.

Whether personal or collective, storms triggered by cumulative effects remind us of the importance of paying attention to the small things—the minor stresses, the daily frustrations, the unresolved conflicts—that, if left unchecked, can build into something much larger and more destructive. They teach us the value of addressing issues as they arise, rather than allowing them to accumulate and overwhelm us.

In the midst of life's storms, whether they are triggered by sudden events or gradual accumulations, we find comfort and strength in the words of Scripture. Psalm 46:1-3 (ESV) offers a profound message of hope and reassurance:

"God is our refuge and strength, always ready to help in times of trouble. So we will not fear when earthquakes come and the mountains crumble into the sea."

These verses speak directly to the heart of our experience with life's storms. They acknowledge the reality of these storms—the earthquakes that shake our foundations, the mountains that crumble before our eyes—but they also offer a powerful message of faith and trust. In the midst of the chaos, God is our refuge, our sanctuary, and our source of strength. We are not alone in our struggles; there is a divine presence that is always ready to help, to guide, and to sustain us.

The imagery of earthquakes and crumbling mountains is particularly evocative. These are not small, insignificant events; they are cataclysmic, representing the most profound disruptions we can imagine. Yet, even in the face of such overwhelming forces, the psalmist tells us not to fear. Why? Because our refuge is not in the stability of the earth or the permanence of the mountains, our refuge is in God, who is unchanging, eternal, and ever-present.

This passage invites us to embrace a posture of trust and surrender, even in the most turbulent of storms. It reminds us that while we may not be able to control the triggers that set these storms in motion, we can always turn to God for refuge and strength. In doing so, we find the courage to face whatever comes our way, knowing that we are supported by a power greater than ourselves.

As we delve deeper into the nature of life's triggers, we enter a realm that transcends the physical and the tangible, touching upon the metaphysical and the spiritual. What is it about these triggers that give them such power over our lives? Why do they have the ability to disrupt our equilibrium, to set in motion storms that can alter the course of our existence?

At a metaphysical level, life's triggers can be seen as the catalysts for spiritual growth and transformation. They are the mechanisms by which the universe prompts us to evolve, to move beyond our current state of being, and to step into a higher level of consciousness. In this sense, triggers are not just random events; they are divinely orchestrated opportunities for us to awaken to deeper truths about ourselves and the world around us.

Consider, for example, the experience of loss. On the surface, loss is a painful and often devastating event. But from a metaphysical perspective, loss can also be seen as a doorway to a deeper understanding of life's impermanence and the nature of attachment. It forces us to confront the reality that nothing in this world is permanent, and that everything we hold dear is ultimately transitory. In this way, loss becomes a teacher, guiding us toward a greater appreciation of the present moment and a deeper connection with the eternal.

Similarly, the experience of betrayal, while deeply wounding, can also serve as a catalyst for spiritual awakening. Betrayal challenges us to examine our relationships, our expectations, and our sense of self-worth. It forces us to confront the illusions we may have been holding onto—the illusion of control, the illusion of security, the illusion of others' infallibility. In the aftermath of betrayal, we may find ourselves stripped of these illusions, left with nothing but the raw, unvarnished truth of our own being. This truth, while difficult to face, is the foundation upon which true spiritual growth is built.

Even the most seemingly mundane triggers—those daily frustrations, minor setbacks, and small disappointments—have their place in the metaphysical landscape of our lives. Each of these triggers is an invitation to pause, to reflect, and to realign with our higher purpose. They remind us that life is not just a series of random events, but a carefully woven tapestry of experiences, each thread contributing to the whole.

In this light, the triggers that set life's storms in motion are not to be feared or avoided, but embraced as opportunities for growth. They challenge us to move beyond our comfort zones, to face our fears, and to trust in the process of life, even when it leads us into the heart of the storm.

As we navigate the storms triggered by life's events, we embark on a spiritual journey—a journey that takes us deep into the heart of our own being, where we confront our deepest fears, our most profound doubts, and our most cherished illusions. It is a path marked by twists and turns, by moments of darkness and light, by periods of intense struggle, and moments of profound peace.

In the midst of the storm, we may feel lost, adrift in a sea of uncertainty. We may question our faith, our purpose, and our place in the world. We may feel as though the storm will never end, that we will be overwhelmed by its force. But it is precisely in these moments of doubt and fear that the true spiritual work begins.

The storm, in all its ferocity, is a crucible—a place of transformation where the old is burned away, and the new is forged. It is in the storm that we are tested, that our faith is challenged, and that our resilience is honed. It is in the storm that we learn what we are truly made of, that we discover the strength that lies within us, and that we deepen our connection with the divine.

As we journey through the storm, we may find ourselves drawn to practices that help us navigate the tumult—prayer, meditation, journaling, or simply spending time in nature. These practices become our anchors, our lifelines in the midst of the chaos. They help us to center ourselves, to find peace amidst the turmoil, and to connect with the still, small voice within that guides us through the storm.

In the end, the storm is not something to be feared but embraced as a sacred part of the spiritual journey. It is a reminder that life is not static but dynamic, that growth requires change, and that transformation often comes through the most challenging experiences. It is a call to trust in the process, to have faith in the unfolding of our lives, and to know that, no matter how fierce the storm, we are never alone.

As we reflect on the nature of life's challenges and the storms they stir within us, we gain a deeper understanding of their significance in our spiritual journey. These challenges, whether arriving as sudden shocks or gradual build-ups, are the universe's way of urging us to awaken, grow, and evolve. Far from being random, they are divinely guided opportunities for us to step into our true potential.

In this light, the storms of life are not merely challenges to be endured but sacred encounters with the divine. They are the moments when we are invited to confront our fears, to let go of our illusions, and to embrace the truth of who we are.

As we move forward on our journey, let us remember the wisdom of Psalm 46:1-3: "God is our refuge and strength, always ready to help in times of trouble. So we will not fear when earthquakes come and the mountains crumble into the sea." These words remind us that, no matter how fierce the storm, we are never alone. There is always a refuge to be found, a source of strength that will carry us through.

In the end, the triggers that set life's storms in motion are not to be feared but embraced as opportunities for growth and transformation. They are the catalysts that propel us forward on our spiritual journey, challenging us to rise to new heights of understanding, wisdom, and compassion. And as we weather these storms, we come to know ourselves more deeply, to trust in the process of life, and to find peace in the midst of the tempest.

Chapter 5:

The Mature Stage

In life, the most challenging storms are not the ones that come unexpectedly, but those that peak after we have already been enduring them for what seems like an eternity. The mature stage of any storm—whether emotional, spiritual, or physical—marks the moment when we are confronted by the full force of the tempest. This stage is not merely an external event but an intense personal confrontation, where we are forced to reckon with the depths of our inner landscape and the limits of our endurance. The mature storm, like a crescendo in a symphony, challenges us to hold steady as the world around us seemingly collapses under the weight of chaos.

This stage of the storm is the peak. It's when everything has come to the stage of overwhelming circumstance. The storm has reached a point where coping mechanisms are no longer just optional; they are essential for survival. This is the moment when your internal resources, emotional reserves, and mental endurance are stretched to their limits, demanding that you find a way to move forward, even in the face of overwhelming odds.

Your life, in these moments, is no longer a reflection of your preferences but rather a reflection of your priorities. Your well-being must be the priority above all else—before circumstance, before situation, before family, friends, or loved ones. In the midst of the storm, you are the priority. One of the most valuable lessons I learned in my experience with personal storms is that I had to put myself first. I had to prioritize understanding myself—my triggers, my emotions, my responses—so I could find peace and become whole. Only by being whole could I navigate the storm effectively and emerge stronger.

This chapter explores the nature of these mature storms, their emotional and psychological toll, and the importance of resilience. We will examine how our immediate responses shape our journey through these storms, discussing real-life examples of individuals who have faced the full brunt of life's challenges. Finally, we will delve into the spiritual dimension of waiting, trusting, and renewing our strength in the midst of adversity.

When life reaches this peak of intensity, coping mechanisms become essential not only for survival but also for healing. A critical part of this process is self-reflection. Talking things through and thinking them through becomes a vital aspect of navigating the storm. We ask ourselves, "What got me here? How can I find a way forward?" These questions aren't just practical—they become a way to reclaim control over our internal state when everything external feels beyond reach.

Self-awareness is key. The storm forces you to pause, reflect, and ultimately understand yourself better. It's during these moments that you begin to understand the value of "you." It's when you realize that peacemaking—within yourself, your emotions, and your mind—is necessary. Before you can fix the external, you have to bring peace to your inner world. You have to use everything you've got to liberate yourself from the turmoil within. The storm becomes a teacher that pushes you to prioritize your emotional health.

One of the key lessons I learned while enduring storms is that our immediate responses often come from impulse. There's a study that reveals we live in a "frontal lobe society," meaning that the frontal lobe, which controls our impulses, is highly active in our everyday lives. In storms, this part of the brain can dominate, causing us to react impulsively—whether through anger, avoidance, or other short-term coping mechanisms.

But coping through impulse alone isn't sustainable. It provides temporary relief at best and often exacerbates the storm's effects in the long run. I had to mature to a place where I could function not from impulse but from understanding that everything is solvable. There are two main ways that things can be solved in a storm. The first is within your power—meaning you have the ability to control and navigate certain aspects of the storm. The second involves circumstances beyond your power to control. However, just because something is outside of your control does not mean it can't be solved. Some things you must allow to play out without your direct intervention, learning to trust the process rather than force solutions.

In both the natural and metaphysical sense, storms build in intensity before they dissipate. The mature stage represents this peak—a culmination of forces that stretch us beyond what we believed was possible. This stage is characterized by an overwhelming intensity. The storm no longer feels like an isolated event but an all-encompassing force that affects every aspect of life: physically, emotionally, and spiritually. At this point, life no longer resembles its calm state; everything is in upheaval, and the weight of the storm seems almost unbearable.

The mature stage of a storm is not just about the external chaos we face. It is also a profound internal experience, where our emotional, psychological, and spiritual reserves are fully tested. The external pressure mirrors an inner tempest, forcing us to confront fears, doubts, and unresolved wounds that may have been dormant for years. The winds of change howl around us, and it feels as if everything that once was secure is now fragile. The ground beneath our feet shifts, leaving us disoriented, confused, and anxious.

Emotionally, the mature stage may manifest as exhaustion, despair, or a sense of helplessness. As the storm rages on, our capacity to cope dwindles, and we begin to question our strength. Spiritually, this stage can be deeply disorienting. Long-held beliefs about security, control, and purpose are often upended, leaving us grappling with existential questions. Why is this happening to me? What purpose could this suffering serve? Where is God in the midst of this turmoil?

Philosophically, the mature stage of a storm can be viewed as the crucible of the human spirit. It is a moment of deep testing, where we are called to redefine what it means to survive—not just in terms of physical or emotional endurance, but in a more profound, spiritual sense. Here, we ask questions that cut to the heart of existence: Who am I in the face of this adversity? What can I learn from this storm? How will I emerge on the other side?

During my own personal storms, I discovered that self-prioritization is not selfish but essential. One of the most important revelations I encountered in my personal storms was the realization that I had to put myself first. I learned that my well-being had to be a priority—before circumstances, situations, or even my loved ones. To truly cope, I needed to be whole within myself. My emotions had to be intact, and I had to understand my triggers. I needed to reflect on why I was reacting in certain ways and what my deeper motivations were.

This shift in focus—prioritizing my own mental, emotional, and spiritual health—allowed me to navigate the storm with more clarity. It became clear that self-awareness is critical. You have to use everything that you have to liberate yourself. You cannot give what you do not have. To be effective for others, you must first ensure that you are whole.

But this stage also offers a paradoxical opportunity. At the very moment when everything seems to be at its breaking point, we are presented with the chance for transformation. The mature stage of the storm, though painful and overwhelming, is where the possibility of true change resides. It is the point at which we are most vulnerable, yet also most open to growth. Like the strongest winds that shape the landscape, the storm shapes us, carving out parts of ourselves that we did not know existed.

At the height of the storm, our instinct is often to survive by any means necessary. Coping mechanisms vary from person to person, but they often include avoidance, denial, or attempts to distract ourselves from the pain. Some people turn to numbing behaviors—whether through substances, excessive work, or emotional withdrawal—to escape the full reality of the storm. Others may react with anger, defiance, or a heightened need for control, as if to will the storm into submission.

However, these reactive coping strategies, though they may provide short-term relief, only prolong our suffering in the long run. Denial of the storm's presence or intensity prevents us from dealing with the root of our pain. Avoidance keeps us stuck, while unhealthy distractions lead us further from the path of healing. Real coping, especially in the mature stage of a storm, begins when we stop running and start facing the storm head-on.

To confront the mature storm requires a shift from reactive coping to proactive resilience. Acceptance is the first step in this process. Acceptance does not mean passivity or resignation to suffering, but rather acknowledging the reality of the storm without resisting it. This is a critical spiritual and psychological turning point. By embracing the storm, we are no longer expending precious energy fighting something that we cannot control. Instead, we can focus on how to endure and grow through the experience.

Surrender is a closely related concept. In the context of storms, surrender is not giving up, but rather letting go of the illusion of control. There is a certain peace that comes from surrendering to the forces at play, trusting that while we may not be able to change the storm, we can change how we respond to it. In many spiritual traditions, surrender is seen as the highest form of faith—a recognition that there are forces greater than ourselves at work, and that our task is not to fight them but to learn from them.

The scripture from Isaiah 40:31 speaks directly to this concept: "But they who wait for the Lord shall renew their strength; they shall mount up with wings like eagles; they shall run and not be weary; they shall walk and not faint." This passage highlights the spiritual importance of waiting, trusting, and renewing one's strength in the midst of the storm. Waiting on the Lord, in this context, is an act of surrender and faith. It is the recognition that, though we are in the storm, renewal will come. It promises that the very winds that batter us can also lift us higher if we have the patience and the trust to wait for that moment.

An important aspect of surviving the storm is realizing that not all battles are meant to be fought. In some instances, the best way forward is to let go. There are forces beyond our control, and to persist in trying to manage them only results in greater exhaustion. Part of enduring the storm is recognizing when to surrender, and trusting that a resolution will come, even if it is not through your direct intervention.

Some circumstances need to run their course, much like a natural storm. You cannot change the wind or the rain, but you can prepare your shelter. This realization can bring a sense of peace, knowing that although you cannot change the storm, you can change how you weather it.

This process of waiting and trusting can be incredibly difficult in the mature stage, where the pressure feels insurmountable. However, true resilience is built through these moments. Resilience is not about avoiding the storm or suppressing our emotions. It is about standing firm in the storm, allowing ourselves to feel the full range of emotions—fear, sorrow, confusion—while trusting that, in time, we will emerge on the other side.

Resilience, at its core, is the ability to endure hardship and emerge from it transformed. In the mature stage of a storm, resilience is not just a matter of surviving; it is about growing stronger through the experience. It is in these moments of profound struggle that we discover the depths of our inner strength—the strength we often didn't know we possessed.

The idea of resilience is deeply intertwined with mental strength, which refers to our capacity to manage our thoughts, emotions, and actions in the face of adversity. Mental strength is not about suppressing emotions or pretending that the storm isn't real. It is about developing the capacity to remain grounded and centered, even as everything around us feels chaotic.

Mental strength is cultivated through intentional practices that build emotional and psychological endurance. One such practice is cultivating a growth mindset—the belief that challenges and difficulties are opportunities for learning and development rather than insurmountable obstacles. When we approach the mature stage of a storm with a growth mindset, we shift our focus from merely enduring the storm to actively seeking the lessons it offers.

Another important aspect of mental strength is self-compassion. In the midst of a storm, it is easy to become self-critical, blaming ourselves for our struggles or believing that we should be handling things better. Self-compassion allows us to extend kindness to ourselves, recognizing that it is human to struggle, to falter, and to feel overwhelmed. It is this gentle self-acceptance that fosters resilience by allowing us to rest and renew our strength, rather than depleting ourselves with harsh self-judgment.

Resilience is also about adaptability—the ability to adjust to new realities and continue moving forward even when life has shifted dramatically. In the mature stage of a storm, adaptability becomes crucial. We may no longer be able to rely on the structures, routines, or supports we once had. The storm demands that we find new ways of coping, new sources of strength, and new pathways forward.

In life, we often cling to what is familiar, even when it no longer serves us. The storm shakes up our sense of normalcy and forces us to adapt. Adaptability is the key to survival, as it allows us to let go of what no longer works and embrace new methods of resilience. Those who adapt not only survive the storm but often come out stronger and more capable of handling future challenges.

Resilience is deeply connected to hope. In the midst of the storm, hope is often the only thing that keeps us moving forward. Hope is not a naïve optimism that denies the reality of suffering, but a steadfast belief that something meaningful can emerge from the pain. Hope is the quiet conviction that, no matter how fierce the storm, it will eventually pass, and we will find a way to rebuild.

History is filled with examples of individuals who have faced the mature stage of life's storms and emerged transformed. These stories remind us that no matter how fierce the storm is, it is possible to endure, and even to thrive.

One powerful example is Viktor Frankl, a Holocaust survivor and the author of Man's Search for Meaning. Frankl endured unimaginable suffering in the concentration camps, yet he emerged with a deep understanding of the human spirit's capacity for resilience. In the midst of the most extreme conditions, he found that the ability to find meaning in suffering was the key to survival. Frankl's philosophy emphasizes that while we cannot always control the external circumstances of our lives, we can control how we respond to them. His story is a testament to the power of resilience in the face of the ultimate storm.

Another example is Malala Yousafzai, who survived an assassination attempt by the Taliban for advocating for girls' education. The physical storm she endured—the gunshot wound to her head—was only part of her journey. The emotional and psychological storm that followed was just as intense. Yet, rather than retreating into fear, Malala chose to use her experience as a platform for change. Her resilience in the face of extreme adversity transformed her into a global advocate for education and human rights, demonstrating the profound strength that can emerge from life's most challenging storms.

In everyday life, there are countless stories of individuals who have faced the mature stage of their own personal storms. These are the people who have lost loved ones, faced debilitating illness, or experienced financial ruin, yet have found a way to rebuild their lives. Their stories remind us that resilience is not just for extraordinary individuals; it is a capacity that exists within each of us.

The scripture from Isaiah 40:31 offers profound wisdom for those navigating the mature stage of life's storms: "But they who wait for the Lord shall renew their strength; they shall mount up with wings like eagles; they shall run and not be weary; they shall walk and not faint." This passage speaks directly to the heart of resilience.

In the storm, waiting can feel like the hardest task of all. We want the storm to end, to find resolution, to move forward. Yet, the scripture teaches that there is strength in waiting—in trusting that there is a divine timing at play, even when we cannot see it. The promise of renewal is not just physical but spiritual. It is a renewal of hope, of purpose, and of faith in the midst of uncertainty.

The image of mounting up with wings like eagles is particularly powerful. Eagles, unlike most birds, do not flee from storms. Instead, they use the wind of the storm to lift them higher. This imagery reminds us that the very forces that seem to threaten us can also be the ones that elevate us to greater heights, if we have the courage and resilience to endure.

The symbolism of the eagle soaring through the storm captures a profound spiritual and philosophical truth: adversity, when faced with courage and resilience, can become the catalyst for our greatest personal and spiritual growth. Just as the eagle does not avoid the storm but instead rises above it, we, too, are invited to harness the energy of life's challenges to elevate ourselves, both mentally and spiritually.

In the midst of a storm, it is natural to want to retreat, to seek shelter, and wait for the storm to pass. However, the eagle shows us a different path. By using the winds of adversity to lift itself higher, it transforms what could be a destructive force into one of empowerment. This imagery reminds us that difficulties, though painful and often overwhelming, carry within them the potential for transformation. The winds that threaten to break us can also be the same forces that propel us toward new insights, strength, and wisdom—if we allow them.

Spiritually, this concept echoes many of the world's great teachings. In Christianity, suffering is often viewed as a path to sanctification, a way to refine the soul and draw closer to the divine. In Buddhism, suffering is seen as an inherent part of life that, once understood and accepted, can lead to enlightenment. Across different traditions, there is a common thread: the storms we face are not meaningless, but opportunities to transcend our current limitations.

In practical terms, this means adopting a mindset that looks for growth within struggle. It requires us to ask, "What can I learn from this?" or "How can this challenge make me stronger?" rather than seeing difficulties only as obstacles. When we do this, we begin to understand that life's storms are not meant to defeat us but to elevate us, much like the eagle that soars above the tempest.

Ultimately, the storm can become our teacher, and the winds that once seemed to tear us down can become the very forces that carry us to new heights. In this way, the imagery of the eagle invites us to trust the process, to find strength in adversity, and to rise above the storm.

Chapter 6:

All That Was Left Unsaid

In the stillness that follows a storm, it is not the absence of sound that one notices first, but rather the heaviness of what remains unsaid. There is a peculiar kind of weight in silence, especially the silence that comes after an upheaval. It is the weight of unfinished conversations, unshed tears, and emotions that were never granted the space to unfold. And it is in this silence that one often feels the full measure of what has been lost.

There is something about the aftermath that demands more from us than the storm itself. During the tempest, we are occupied—by survival, by urgency, by the demands of the moment. We react, we adapt, and we push through, often without thinking. But when the winds have ceased and the waters have receded, we are left with something far more challenging: reflection. It is then that the true nature of what has been endured comes to light, and we find ourselves confronted not just with the physical or emotional toll of the storm, but with the deeper, more elusive impact of all that was left unspoken.

There is a certain irony in the aftermath of a storm. One might expect the calm to bring relief, a sense of closure. But instead, it often feels as though the real storm begins only when the external chaos has ended. The quiet that follows is not peaceful, but thick with tension. It is a quiet that presses inward, making space for the unresolved to surface.

In the natural world, storms pass, leaving behind debris,

broken branches, uprooted trees, and flooded fields. These are visible reminders of the storm's force, evidence of its power and destruction. Yet, in the inner world, the aftermath is far more subtle, but no less devastating. The things that remain unsaid—the apologies never voiced, the fears never admitted, the truths left unspoken—become like invisible scars, shaping the landscape of our souls in ways we do not always understand.

Silence, after all, is not merely the absence of sound. It is a presence all its own, one that can either heal or deepen the wounds left by the storm. When we leave things unsaid, we leave pieces of ourselves behind, fragments of our inner world that linger in the space between what is and what could have been. These unspoken emotions do not simply fade away with time. Instead, they grow, taking root in the quiet, until they become part of the fabric of who we are.

In Psalm 69:14-18, the psalmist cries out, "Deliver me from sinking in the mire; let me be delivered from my enemies and from the deep waters." This is not just a plea for physical salvation, but for release from the internal storms that threaten to pull us under. The mire, in this case, is not merely external; it is the weight of all that remains unresolved within us. The psalmist's plea speaks to the deep human need for expression—for a way to bring forth what lies beneath the surface, before it drowns us entirely.

To leave things unsaid is not simply to withhold words, but to carry a burden. Every unspoken emotion—whether it be anger, sorrow, love, or fear—adds weight to our hearts, until we are no longer certain what is holding us down. We tell ourselves that silence is easier, that it spares us the discomfort of confrontation, the vulnerability of being seen. But in truth, silence is often the heaviest thing we bear.

Consider, for a moment, the nature of unspoken anger. Anger that is voiced can be dealt with; it can be understood, negotiated, or even forgiven. But anger that is left unspoken festers. It does not dissipate, but instead turns inward, transforming into resentment, bitterness, or worse, self-reproach. The same is true of sorrow. Grief that is shared becomes lighter, spread out among those who care for us. But grief that is silenced becomes an anchor, dragging us deeper into the depths of isolation.

And what of love? Even love, if left unspoken, can become a source of pain. The words we do not say to those we care about are often the ones that haunt us the most. We tell ourselves that they already know, that there is no need to speak the obvious. Yet, there is power in expression, a power that goes beyond the mere transmission of information. To say "I love you" is not just to state a fact, but to create a connection, to affirm the bond that exists between two souls. When we withhold these words, we deprive ourselves and others of the intimacy that comes from shared vulnerability.

There is a tendency, particularly in times of crisis, to focus on survival above all else. In the midst of the storm, we do what we must to endure, to keep moving forward. But survival, on its own, is not enough. To truly live, we must also communicate, connect, and express the fullness of our inner worlds. Otherwise, we risk becoming like the debris left behind after the storm—broken, scattered, and incomplete.

Why, then, do we so often resist the very thing that could bring us healing? Why do we leave so much unsaid, even when the opportunity for expression presents itself? Part of the answer lies in fear. To speak, especially in the wake of a storm, is to open oneself up to vulnerability. It is to risk being misunderstood, to face the possibility that our words will not be enough, or worse, that they will reveal more than we intended.

There is also the fear of confrontation. When emotions have been suppressed for too long, the act of bringing them to the surface can feel overwhelming. We fear that once the floodgates are opened, we will not be able to control what comes out. And so, we remain silent, convincing ourselves that it is better this way, that time will heal what we cannot bear to voice.

But time, on its own, does not heal. It merely allows the unspoken to sink deeper, to become more entrenched in our being. What is left unsaid does not simply disappear; it becomes part of the background noise of our lives, influencing our thoughts, our actions, and our relationships in ways we may not even recognize.

To express oneself, then, is not just a matter of communication—it is an act of liberation. When we give voice to our emotions, we release the energy that has been trapped within us, allowing it to move, to transform. This is not always easy, nor is it always comfortable. But it is necessary if we are to heal.

The process of expression is, in many ways, a process of self-revelation. When we speak our truth—whether it be a truth of anger, sorrow, or love—we bring our inner world into the light, where it can be seen, understood, and ultimately integrated. This is not to say that every emotion must be shared with others. Some truths are meant to be spoken only to ourselves, in the quiet of reflection. But even this kind of private expression is vital, for it is through the act of acknowledging our own feelings that we begin to make peace with them.

Healing, in its deepest sense, is not about erasing the scars left by the storm, but about coming to terms with them. It is about understanding that the things we left unsaid were not failures, but part of our human journey. In the aftermath of the storm, we are often tempted to dwell on what we should have said, and what we could have done differently. But this kind of thinking only traps us in the past, preventing us from moving forward.

To heal is not to re-write the past, but to accept it. It is to acknowledge that we did the best we could with the tools we had at the time. The things we left unsaid were not necessarily wrong—they were simply part of our journey toward understanding. And now, in the quiet after the storm, we have the opportunity to revisit those unspoken emotions, not with judgment, but with compassion.

This process of revisiting is not about reliving the pain of the past, but about transforming it. When we bring our unspoken emotions to the surface, we allow them to be seen in a new light. We see them not as burdens, but as opportunities for growth. In this way, healing becomes less about closure and more about integration—about taking the lessons of the storm and allowing them to shape us in ways that make us stronger, wiser, and more compassionate.

It is important to recognize that healing is not a linear process. There will be days when the weight of the unspoken feels too heavy to bear, when the silence seems impenetrable. But there will also be moments of clarity, when the words we need come to us, when the emotions we have buried begin to rise to the surface, not as threats, but as gifts. It is in these moments that we find the courage to speak, to express, to release.

Closure is a word that carries a weight of expectation, often misunderstood as the final step in resolving conflict or healing emotional wounds. Many imagine closure as a clean, definitive end to a chapter—a state where all the loose ends are neatly tied, leaving nothing unresolved. It conjures an image of turning a page and never looking back, of reaching a point where everything has been said, done, and felt, and where peace comes from a total sense of completion.

However, in reality, closure is rarely so simple or tidy. Life, with all its complexities, doesn't always offer us the luxury of perfect endings or neatly wrapped resolutions. Instead, closure is less about finality and more about finding peace amid the unresolved. It is about learning to live with what cannot be changed or fixed, and finding a way to grow and move forward in spite of that.

True closure, especially in the context of the unspoken—those feelings, thoughts, and emotions that linger in the silence—is not about ensuring that every conversation is had or that every emotion is fully voiced. Sometimes, the path to closure lies in recognizing that certain things will remain unsaid and that certain feelings may never be fully shared or understood. And in some cases, this is perfectly okay. It is not always necessary to force closure by saying everything that is on our hearts.

The challenge, however, is in making peace with this reality. We are often tempted to believe that closure can only come when we have fully expressed ourselves or when the other person acknowledges what we feel. But sometimes, the people with whom we need closure may no longer be in our lives, or the opportunity to speak may no longer exist. In these moments, closure is not about the external, but about what happens within us.

We must come to terms with the fact that some chapters in life will remain unfinished, and some conversations will never be had. The key to closure is not in waiting for a perfect moment to voice everything, but in learning to accept that some things may never be said. This acceptance, while difficult, is ultimately freeing. It shifts our focus away from what we cannot change and toward what we can—our own healing and growth.

In this way, closure becomes a deeply personal and internal process. It is not something that happens to us, as if we are passive recipients of it. Rather, it is something we actively create. Closure does not require external validation or perfect timing. It requires a willingness to face the unresolved parts of our lives and find peace within ourselves, even when not everything has been made right or complete. This is not resignation or giving up; it is an act of grace, allowing us to move forward without carrying the burden of unfinished business on our shoulders.

There is a profound spiritual lesson in this understanding of closure. Life is full of unfinished business, unresolved emotions, and unspoken words. It is an inherent part of the human condition. But our task is not to resolve everything. Our role is to do the best we can with what we have, to communicate when we are able, and to forgive ourselves for the times when we cannot. We must recognize that closure is not the result of perfection or of saying everything perfectly at the right moment. It is the result of accepting our limitations and finding peace with what is, rather than what could have been.

In *Psalm 69:14-18*, the psalmist offers a beautiful reflection on this process: "Deliver me from sinking in the mire; let me be delivered from my enemies and from the deep waters. Let not the flood sweep over me, or the deep swallow me up, or the pit close its mouth over me." This plea is not for the storm to be undone, or for every wrong to be righted. Instead, it is a prayer for resilience—for the strength to withstand the uncertainty, the unfinished, and the unresolved. The psalmist does not ask for the flood to disappear but for the ability to stand firm in its midst.

This is the essence of closure: not erasing the storms of life, but finding the inner strength to face them. It is about trusting that we do not need to resolve everything perfectly in order to move forward. The unspoken, the unfinished, the unresolved—they are part of the fabric of life. What matters is not that we tie every loose end, but that we find peace in the process, that we learn to navigate the deep waters with grace and resilience. Closure, then, is not about achieving a perfect ending but about finding the courage to live peacefully with what remains unfinished.

In the end, the things we leave unsaid are not failures, but opportunities. Too often, we perceive silence as an inadequacy, as if our inability or reluctance to voice certain thoughts or emotions marks a kind of personal shortcoming. Yet, to view the unspoken purely through the lens of failure is to miss the deeper significance of silence. What remains unsaid is not merely the absence of expression, but a fertile ground for introspection and growth. These unsaid words and unexpressed feelings are opportunities for us to turn inward, to examine the parts of ourselves that we may not fully understand. In that space, we learn to listen—not only to the outer world but to the subtle, often neglected, voice within ourselves.

Silence, then, becomes a tool for deeper listening. It is not simply about waiting for the right moment to speak but learning to hear what lies beneath the surface. So much of modern life is dominated by noise—literal and metaphorical. The constant hum of activity, conversation, media, and distractions fill our days and drown out the quieter, more reflective aspects of our inner life. We live in a world that values quick responses and immediate action, often at the expense of thoughtful reflection. In the noise of everyday life, it is easy to overlook the spaces where true healing and understanding can occur.

It is only in silence, when the noise recedes, that we begin to hear the deeper currents of our own being. Silence provides the time and space to sit with what has been left unsaid, not to correct or fix it, but to understand it. These unsaid things are markers of where we are in our personal journey. They show us the places where we are still hesitant, where we fear vulnerability, or where we are not yet ready to fully open ourselves to the world. They also show us where we need to grow, to love, to forgive—not just others but ourselves.

The silence after the storm is not an empty space, but a sacred one. In the aftermath of life's challenges, there is a tendency to rush toward resolution. We feel a need to quickly rebuild, to fill the void left by the storm with action, with movement, with noise. But silence is not something to be filled; it is something to be honored. It is within this sacred quiet that we are invited to sit with our own hearts, to feel the weight of the unspoken, and to choose, consciously, how we will move forward. It is an invitation to slow down, to embrace the stillness rather than resist it, and in doing so, to allow our true selves to emerge.

In this space, we are not avoiding or escaping the unresolved emotions but acknowledging them in a way that words often cannot. Silence can serve as a bridge between the intellect and the heart, between what we think we know and what we feel at a deeper, more intuitive level. When we allow ourselves to sit in the quiet after the storm, we begin to recognize that not everything needs to be resolved in the ways we initially imagined. The healing that takes place in silence is different from the kind of healing we find in conversation or action. It is less about fixing and more about accepting—accepting that some things cannot be changed, that some emotions will never be fully understood or articulated, and that this, too, is a part of our human experience.

Will we allow the silence to consume us, or will we use it as a bridge to deeper understanding? This is a question we must ask ourselves, for silence, like any powerful force, can either isolate or enlighten. If we approach silence with fear—if we see it as a void to be feared, a reminder of all that is incomplete or unresolved—it can become overwhelming. But if we see silence as an opportunity, as a space in which we can reconnect with ourselves and with the deeper truths of life, then it becomes a source of strength. Silence, in this sense, is not something that happens to us but something we engage with. It is an active process, one that requires intention and openness.

In this silence, there is a kind of truth that cannot be found in the noise of everyday life. It is a truth that speaks not in words, but in presence. In the rush of daily life, we often confuse talking with communicating and noise with understanding. We fill the air with words, hoping they will bridge the gap between ourselves and others, but often, it is in the silence between words that the most profound communication takes place. The truth of who we are— beneath the surface, beneath the unspoken—exists in this space. It is a truth that we cannot always express in words because it transcends language. It is the essence of our being, the core of our identity, the quiet knowing that remains even when everything else falls away.

And it is here, in this sacred quiet, that we find the courage to heal. Healing is not always loud or dramatic. Often, it is subtle, quiet, and slow. It unfolds in the moments when we allow ourselves to sit in silence, to feel the fullness of what has been left unsaid, and to recognize that there is nothing we need to do to make it better. The mere act of being present with ourselves—with our own unspoken thoughts and emotions—is enough to begin the healing process. In silence, we give ourselves permission to be as we are, without the need to explain or justify.

Let the silence be not a burden, but a guide. There is wisdom in silence, if we are willing to listen. Let it lead you to the places where the unspoken can finally be heard, not necessarily in the form of words but in the form of understanding. The emotions you have buried, the thoughts you have suppressed, will rise to the surface, not as overwhelming forces but as gentle reminders of what still needs attention. It is in this transformation—this shift from avoidance to acceptance—that we find our way forward. Silence is not a dead end, but a path—a path that leads us not just out of the storm, but into the light of a new day.

In this light, we begin to see that silence is not the absence of communication but a deeper, more profound form of it. It is in the quiet that we truly hear ourselves, that we learn to listen to the subtle whispers of our soul, and that we find the courage to be present with what is. Silence teaches us that healing does not always come from speaking but from sitting with the unsaid and allowing it to transform us from within.

The things we leave unsaid are not failures but opportunities—opportunities to listen more deeply, to ourselves and to others. In the end, it is not about finding the perfect words or the perfect resolution, but about embracing the quiet acceptance of what is. And it is in this acceptance that we find the path forward, a path illuminated not by noise or action, but by the quiet, steady light of presence.

71

Chapter 7:

Why am I here?

This is not a question of "LIFE"—it's more a question of circumstance. This is one of those instances where seeking out the "why" is beneficial to understanding. Understanding helps to disconnect and expose the reasons behind the storms we face. What led to the storms? Was it learned behaviors, reoccurring patterns, or cycles passed down through generations? These reflections are essential, especially when we find ourselves burdened to be the blueprint—to break generational curses that have weighed on our families and ourselves.

We endure these storms because sometimes, we're meant to be the ones who challenge and end these cycles. We are tested so our lives can become blueprints or testimonies of how to overcome. These "L's" we take—whether losses or lessons—are vital. Discovering the lessons within the storm or identifying the learning piece helps us avoid repeating patterns in future cycles. It prevents us from becoming repeat offenders, from running into the same brick walls repeatedly. After all, no one wants to keep re-testing on the same lessons.

In the midst of life's inevitable storms, it's natural to reflect on deeper questions about existence and purpose. "Why am I here?" This question, though often asked in times of distress, is universal and touches the core of our human experience. It isn't just about finding a reason to endure the storms, but about seeking a deeper understanding of our purpose—how our personal journey fits into the broader tapestry of life. By embracing self-reflection and spiritual wisdom, we can begin to see our place and purpose with clearer eyes, even when surrounded by uncertainty.

When challenges arise, it is tempting to view them as purely negative disruptions, yet they can serve as profound opportunities for growth and reflection. Life's storms, whether they come in the form of personal loss, uncertainty, or change, often force us to stop and consider not only what we are experiencing but why we are going through it. They challenge our preconceived notions about who we are and what we're meant to do. The turbulence shakes the foundation of our everyday life, clearing the space for deeper introspection. We find ourselves grappling with questions of purpose, seeking to understand if there is meaning in the struggles we face.

At these moments, self-reflection becomes not just a tool but a necessity. The process of self-reflection pushes us to examine our core beliefs, values, and aspirations. It asks us to look inward and consider how we've been navigating life's journey. Are we moving in alignment with our true selves, or have we been caught up in external expectations, drifting further from our authentic path? This is where the true power of reflection comes in—not just in finding answers but in rediscovering the essence of who we are amidst the storm.

Spiritual wisdom, whether drawn from religious teachings, philosophical principles, or personal meditation, offers vital insights during these times. Throughout history, spiritual traditions have emphasized the importance of finding meaning in adversity. They remind us that life's trials are not arbitrary but are often essential to our growth. In many traditions, storms are seen as metaphors for transformation—necessary disruptions that pave the way for renewal. They challenge us to evolve, encouraging us to strip away distractions and focus on what truly matters.

Take, for example, the concept of resilience. In many spiritual teachings, resilience is not just about surviving hardship, but about thriving in the face of it. It's about finding strength, not despite the storm, but because of it. Each challenge offers the possibility of deepening our understanding of ourselves and the world. Storms become catalysts for discovering inner strength we may not have known existed. They invite us to confront our fears and doubts, to ask ourselves difficult questions about our purpose, and to grow in ways we didn't anticipate.

Part of the search for purpose also involves the recognition that our journey is part of a much larger narrative. We are not isolated beings, disconnected from the world around us; rather, we are part of a vast and interconnected web of life. Our struggles, successes, and growth all have ripple effects. Understanding our place in this larger context gives our personal journey a sense of meaning beyond the immediate. This perspective shifts the focus from "Why is this happening to me?" to "What can I learn from this, and how can I use this experience to contribute to the greater good?"

This broader view is important when considering our role in life's storms. Sometimes, the answer to "Why am I here?" lies not just in self-discovery, but in understanding how our journey influences and supports others. Our challenges, though deeply personal, often mirror the experiences of those around us. By overcoming adversity, we don't just grow ourselves; we become a source of strength, empathy, and guidance for others who may face similar storms. In this way, our purpose is intertwined with the purpose of those around us, deepening our sense of connection and meaning.

The pursuit of purpose during life's storms also leads us to contemplate the legacy we wish to leave behind. While life's challenges can make us feel small and powerless, they are also opportunities to reflect on the impact we want to have on the world. How do we want to be remembered? What do we want to contribute to the lives of those we encounter? The storms we face often clarify our values, forcing us to focus on what is truly important and guiding us toward actions that reflect our deepest convictions.

In the end, life's storms may not always provide immediate clarity, but they do offer the space for profound reflection and transformation. "Why am I here?" becomes less of a question to fear and more of an invitation to explore. The storms we face are not just obstacles to overcome but opportunities to realign ourselves with our true purpose, to discover the deeper meaning behind our journey, and to connect more fully with the world around us.

By embracing both self-reflection and spiritual wisdom, we open ourselves to understanding our purpose on a deeper level. We recognize that our existence is not random, that the challenges we face are part of a greater process of growth, and that our place in the world is both unique and significant.

Even amidst life's greatest uncertainties, this clarity offers a guiding light, reminding us that the journey itself, though often difficult, is rich with purpose and meaning.

At the heart of our existence is our self-concept—the perception we hold of ourselves, our abilities, and our worth. It is the lens through which we view the world and navigate our life. Self-efficacy, the belief in our ability to influence and shape our environment, also plays a vital role in how we confront challenges. Both of these attributes, self-concept, and self-efficacy, determine not only how we handle adversity but also how we see our place in the world.

When life's storms hit, our self-concept is often shaken. We may find ourselves questioning our value or doubting our ability to cope. This internal struggle is natural and provides a moment for reflection—an opportunity to ask, "Who am I in the face of this storm?" and "What am I capable of?" These moments of self-questioning are crucial because they reveal the strength or fragility of our self-concept.

Self-efficacy, on the other hand, represents our internal power to shape the outcomes of our lives. When we believe that we have some level of control over the circumstances we face, we are more likely to engage with challenges constructively. Even if the storm is beyond our control, our belief in our capacity to navigate through it allows us to persevere. When we ask, "Why am I here?" during moments of hardship, we are not just seeking an existential answer, but a confirmation of our ability to survive and thrive in the face of adversity.

Jeremiah 29:11 (NIV) reminds us of the divine assurance that there is a greater purpose at work: "For I know the plans I have for you," declares the Lord, "plans to prosper you and not to harm you, plans to give you hope and a future." This promise of hope is crucial when we confront our own doubts and fears. It suggests that even when we feel insignificant or overwhelmed by life's challenges, there is a divine purpose guiding us forward. This spiritual truth can strengthen our self-concept, reaffirming that we are not simply at the mercy of life's storms but active participants in a larger divine plan.

Thus, understanding self-concept and building self-efficacy are not merely psychological exercises—they are spiritual acts of affirmation. They help us recognize our worth, our ability to endure, and our unique role in the unfolding story of life. When we anchor our identity in these truths, we develop resilience, enabling us to face life's storms with grace and confidence.

Understanding what triggers our emotional responses is a crucial part of self-awareness, especially when we are weathering personal storms. Each of us carries emotional baggage from past experiences, and during times of stress, these hidden wounds may be activated. By identifying these triggers, we can prevent ourselves from being overwhelmed by emotions and instead take conscious control of our reactions.

Personal triggers can come from past trauma, unresolved conflicts, or even unmet expectations. For instance, a person who has experienced rejection in their childhood may find that certain interactions in adulthood stir up feelings of inadequacy or fear of abandonment. Recognizing these triggers is the first step to emotional mastery. When we understand the source of our emotional reactions, we gain the power to navigate them skillfully rather than be consumed by them.

Navigating emotions is a process that requires practice and patience. It is easy to get swept away by the intensity of our feelings, but emotions, like the weather, pass. During life's storms, our emotions may fluctuate wildly—fear, anger, sadness, or confusion may arise without warning. However, with mindful attention, we can learn to observe our emotions without being overwhelmed by them.

There are several strategies that can help us manage emotions during these times:

• **Mindfulness and Meditation**: By learning to observe our thoughts and feelings without judgment, we can create a mental space where we can choose our responses rather than react impulsively.

• **Self-Compassion**: Treating ourselves with kindness, especially when we are emotionally vulnerable, allows us to process difficult feelings without falling into self-criticism or despair.

• **Prayer and Reflection**: Turning to spiritual practices can ground us during emotional turbulence. Through prayer, we can seek divine guidance and comfort, anchoring ourselves in faith and trusting in a higher power to carry us through.

The ability to navigate emotions is essential in

answering the question, "Why am I here?" because it connects us to our deeper selves. When we understand our emotional landscape, we begin to see how our reactions to life's storms shape our journey. Emotions are not to be feared or suppressed, but embraced as part of our human experience. They provide insight into our inner world, showing us where healing and growth are needed.

In every storm, there is an internal battle between the mind and external circumstances. Often, the turmoil we experience is not solely due to the events unfolding around us, but how our minds interpret and respond to those events. This internal battle—our mind versus our circumstances—determines whether we will be defeated by the storm or rise above it.

The mind is a powerful instrument, capable of creating peace or generating chaos depending on where we place our focus. During a crisis, our minds are naturally drawn to thoughts of fear, doubt, and anxiety. These thoughts can quickly spiral out of control, leading us to feel powerless against the circumstances we face. However, as spiritual teachings remind us, the storm outside does not have to dictate the storm within.

The internal battle often involves the choice between faith and fear. In moments of despair, fear can feel all-consuming. We may find ourselves fixated on worst-case scenarios, unable to see beyond the immediate challenges. However, we also have the power to choose faith—a belief that despite the chaos, there is a path forward, guided by divine providence.

Philippians 4:8 (NIV) encourages us to focus on what is true, noble, and right, reminding us that we have the power to direct our thoughts: "Finally, brothers and sisters, whatever is true, whatever is noble, whatever is right, whatever is pure, whatever is lovely, whatever is admirable—if anything is excellent or praiseworthy—think about such things." This shift in focus does not deny the reality of our difficulties, but it reorients our mind toward hope and positivity, giving us the strength to persevere.

When we understand that the true battle is within, we gain a sense of control over our experience. External circumstances may be beyond our control, but our thoughts and attitudes are not. By focusing on what is within our power—our thoughts, our reactions, and our mindset—we create an inner sanctuary of peace that allows us to withstand life's storms. This inner shift is not just about surviving difficult moments but learning to thrive amidst them.

Adversity, though painful, often leads to profound self-discovery. When we face challenges, we are forced to confront the question, "Why am I here?" in a way that goes beyond surface-level understanding. In the midst of a storm, life's distractions fall away, leaving us to grapple with the essence of who we are and what we are meant to do. It is through this process that we often find clarity and purpose.

One of the great paradoxes of life is that our most profound growth often arises from our most difficult experiences. Adversity strips away the superficial layers of our identity, revealing the core of our being. When everything is uncertain, we are given the opportunity to discover what is truly important. This process of refinement, though uncomfortable, is necessary for our spiritual evolution.

In the spiritual sense, adversity serves as a teacher. Just as metal is purified through fire, our character is shaped through hardship. The Bible offers numerous examples of individuals who found their purpose through adversity. Take, for instance, Joseph, whose life was marked by betrayal, slavery, and imprisonment. Yet, through his trials, Joseph ultimately rose to a position of great power and was able to save his family from famine. His story illustrates that even when our circumstances seem bleak, they may be preparing us for a greater purpose.

Adversity also teaches us empathy. When we have experienced suffering, we become more attuned to the suffering of others. Our pain becomes a bridge of connection, allowing us to offer compassion and support to those who are facing similar struggles. In this way, our personal storms serve not only our own growth but also the growth of those around us.

The transformative power of adversity lies in our ability to find meaning in our suffering. Viktor Frankl, a Holocaust survivor and psychiatrist, famously wrote about the importance of finding meaning in even the most difficult circumstances. In his work *Man's Search for Meaning*, Frankl observed that those who could find a sense of purpose in their suffering were more likely to survive and thrive, even in the most extreme conditions. This idea echoes the biblical promise that "God works for the good of those who love him, who have been called according to his purpose" (Romans 8:28, NIV).

When we approach adversity with a sense of curiosity—asking not only "Why am I here?" but "What is this teaching me?"—we open ourselves to the possibility of transformation. Our pain, rather than being a burden, becomes a source of strength and wisdom, guiding us toward a deeper understanding of our purpose.

Throughout history, scripture has served as a guiding light for those navigating the storms of life. In particular, Jeremiah 29:11 offers a powerful reminder of hope and divine purpose: "For I know the plans I have for you," declares the Lord, "plans to prosper you and not to harm you, plans to give you hope and a future." This verse serves as a spiritual anchor, reminding us that no matter how overwhelming the storm is, there is a divine plan at work in our lives.

The assurance that God has a plan for each of us provides a sense of comfort and direction. It reminds us that our lives are not random, and that the difficulties we face are not without meaning. Even when we cannot see the full picture, we can trust that there is a greater purpose unfolding, one that is ultimately for our good.

Trusting in this divine plan requires faith, especially when the storm is fierce, and the future seems uncertain. Yet, it is precisely in these moments of uncertainty that faith becomes most powerful. Faith allows us to surrender our need for control and to trust that there is a higher power guiding us toward the fulfillment of our purpose.

The question, "Why am I here?" is not one that can be answered in a single moment or a single chapter. It is a question that we carry with us throughout our lives, one that evolves as we grow and change. However, as we navigate life's storms, we begin to uncover pieces of the answer. Each storm reveals a little more about who we are, what we are capable of, and the purpose that we are here to fulfill.

By embracing self-reflection, understanding our emotional triggers, and engaging in the internal battle between mind and circumstances, we gain clarity on our purpose. We learn that adversity is not something to be feared but something to be embraced, for it is through adversity that we are refined and strengthened.

As we continue on our journey, let us hold onto the promise of Jeremiah 29:11, trusting that there is a plan for each of us—a plan for hope and a future. Though the storms of life may be fierce, they are temporary. What endures is the strength we build, the lessons we learn, and the purpose we fulfill as we walk through them.

Adversity, though painful, often leads to profound self-discovery. When we face challenges, we are forced to confront the question, "Why am I here?" in a way that goes beyond surface-level understanding. In the midst of a storm, life's distractions fall away, leaving us to grapple with the essence of who we are and what we are meant to do. It is through this process that we often find clarity and purpose.

One of the great paradoxes of life is that our most profound growth often arises from our most difficult experiences. Adversity strips away the superficial layers of our identity, revealing the core of our being. When everything is uncertain, we are given the opportunity to discover what is truly important. This process of refinement, though uncomfortable, is necessary for our spiritual evolution.

In the spiritual sense, adversity serves as a teacher. Just as metal is purified through fire, our character is shaped through hardship. The Bible offers numerous examples of individuals who found their purpose through adversity. Take, for instance, Joseph, whose life was marked by betrayal, slavery, and imprisonment. Yet, through his trials, Joseph ultimately rose to a position of great power and was able to save his family from famine. His story illustrates that even when our circumstances seem bleak, they may be preparing us for a greater purpose.

Adversity also teaches us empathy. When we have experienced suffering, we become more attuned to the suffering of others. Our pain becomes a bridge of connection, allowing us to offer compassion and support to those who are facing similar struggles. In this way, our personal storms serve not only our own growth but also the growth of those around us.

The transformative power of adversity lies in our ability to find meaning in our suffering. Viktor Frankl, a Holocaust survivor and psychiatrist, famously wrote about the importance of finding meaning in even the most difficult circumstances. In his work *Man's Search for Meaning*, Frankl observed that those who could find a sense of purpose in their suffering were more likely to survive and thrive, even in the most extreme conditions. This idea echoes the biblical promise that "God works for the good of those who love him, who have been called according to his purpose"

(Romans 8:28, NIV).

When we approach adversity with a sense of curiosity—asking not only "Why am I here?" but "What is this teaching me?"—we open ourselves to the possibility of transformation. Our pain, rather than being a burden, becomes a source of strength and wisdom, guiding us toward a deeper understanding of our purpose.

Chapter 8:
The You, You Need to Know

In life, our greatest challenge and responsibility is not simply to survive or overcome external challenges but to truly understand and connect with the essence of who we are. The journey of self-discovery is perhaps the most profound adventure we can embark on because it requires delving into the unseen realms of the self, confronting fears, and embracing both strengths and weaknesses. This chapter explores the intricate process of self-discovery, practices for personal growth, and the critical importance of aligning one's actions with core values for a life of authenticity.

Guarding our peace and grounding ourselves in the chaos of daily life is essential to the journey of self-discovery. This grounding helps us to create a clear separation between what happens to us and who we are at our core. By learning how to maintain this separation, we can cultivate an inner resilience that allows us to navigate life with wisdom and perspective, rather than reacting impulsively to every external stimulus. This idea echoes Ecclesiastes 1:9 (NKJV): "That which has been is what will be, that which is done is what will be done." Recognizing that challenges may recur, we are reminded that growth is cyclical; we will continually be tested in ways that reveal our progress, areas for improvement, and our spiritual preparedness.

There are times when responding does not help, and in those moments, choosing stillness over reaction can guard our peace. When we guard our inner peace, we allow ourselves the space to listen to our true selves, free from the influence of external chaos. This choice not only preserves our mental and emotional well-being but also aligns us more closely with God's desire for us to walk in peace and clarity.

The dissipating stage of self-discovery is when we begin to release old identities, harmful beliefs, or fears that may have once served us but now hold us back. It is a time for us to assess what we need to let go of to make room for new growth and transformation. Just as we let go of what no longer serves us, we also prepare ourselves for future storms with renewed wisdom. Recognizing that life's challenges may persist, we learn to build internal strength and faith, so that when the storms return, we are prepared to face them with courage and peace. In this way, self-discovery is not only a process of knowing ourselves better but also of becoming resilient, wise, and prepared for what lies ahead.

The essence of self-discovery goes beyond surface-level understanding; it calls us to look deeper, into the soul, where the storms of life cannot reach. It demands that we confront the parts of ourselves that are often hidden from public view—our insecurities, vulnerabilities, and even the parts of us shaped by trauma or societal expectations. Psalm 23:2-4 (ESV) offers an encouraging backdrop for this inner journey: "He leads me beside still waters. He restores my soul. He leads me in paths of righteousness for His name's sake." This scripture emphasizes the restorative power of faith, guiding us toward peace, authenticity, and wholeness. The restoration of the soul, as mentioned here, is not just a spiritual promise; it is also a call for self-reflection, internal alignment, and genuine understanding of the self.

The Process of Self-Discovery and Personal Growth

Self-discovery is more than a personal hobby or interest; it is a necessary foundation for meaningful living. Many of us go through life reacting to the external circumstances around us—family obligations, societal expectations, or career demands—without fully engaging with our internal compass. The challenge lies in shifting from this reactive mode to a proactive engagement with our inner selves. Personal growth begins when we stop living by default and instead begin to intentionally seek answers to life's deeper questions: Who am I, really? What do I value most in life? How can I align my actions with my core beliefs?

The journey of self-discovery can be likened to peeling back the layers of an onion. On the surface, we find our everyday behaviors, preferences, and roles. Beneath that are the values we hold dear and the emotional landscapes we inhabit. Deeper still lie our fears, wounds, and unresolved traumas. The most profound layer—the core of our being— is where we uncover our truest self, the part of us untouched by external circumstances or egoic desires.

This process of uncovering our true selves requires patience, vulnerability, and the willingness to confront aspects of ourselves that we may have been avoiding. It is often in the quiet moments—away from the demands of daily life—that we begin to hear the whispers of our soul. As we embark on this journey, we must be prepared to encounter both light and shadow, both beauty and discomfort. Growth often comes from facing the parts of ourselves we least want to acknowledge.

Personal growth is not a linear process. It is cyclical and continuous, often involving periods of reflection, transformation, and integration. During times of reflection, we become aware of the patterns, beliefs, and behaviors that have shaped us. Transformation occurs when we actively seek to change those patterns that no longer serve us, and integration is the process of embodying our newfound insights into our daily lives. As Psalm 23:2-4 (ESV) reminds us, "He leads me beside still waters. He restores my soul. He leads me in paths of righteousness for his name's sake." The restoration of the soul is not merely a passive event but a divine process of aligning ourselves with a higher purpose, where personal growth and spiritual maturity become intertwined.

The process of self-discovery is not just about intellectual understanding; it is also a spiritual journey. It invites us to recognize the divine within us—the imago Dei, the image of God, that we carry. To know ourselves is to know God more fully, as we are reflections of His creation. As we grow in self-awareness, we grow in our ability to fulfill our divine purpose.

Tools and Practices for Knowing Oneself Better

Self-discovery does not happen by accident. It requires intentional practices that help us uncover the depths of our being and reveal the truths we may have buried beneath layers of societal conditioning or emotional defense mechanisms. The following tools and practices can help guide us on this transformative journey:

1. **Journaling as a Spiritual and Emotional Compass:** Journaling is one of the most effective ways to externalize our internal world. It serves as both a reflective practice and a spiritual exercise. By writing down our thoughts, feelings, and experiences, we create a space for self-exploration and healing. Journaling allows us to track our emotional patterns and habitual responses, offering insights into our deeper motivations and fears. The act of writing becomes a dialogue with the soul, an opportunity to ask: "What is God trying to teach me in this moment? How can I live more authentically?"

Journaling can also serve as a form of prayer. By incorporating scripture or spiritual prompts into our writing, we can align our reflections with divine guidance. For example, writing about how Psalm 23 applies to our current emotional state can help us better understand where we need restoration and peace. Over time, journaling reveals patterns that may not be immediately visible. It can highlight the recurring themes of our lives—our struggles, aspirations, and moments of divine intervention—helping us to see how God is working in and through us.

Additionally, journaling fosters emotional release. When we give ourselves the freedom to write without judgment, we often uncover emotions we have suppressed. Whether it is anger, sadness, or fear, journaling allows us to express these feelings in a safe space, releasing them in a healthy way rather than letting them fester within. The process of writing helps us process our emotions and gain clarity on how they shape our actions.

2. **Meditation and Mindfulness:** Meditation is a

practice of turning inward, quieting the mind, and becoming present in the moment. In meditation, we create space to hear the voice of our true self, which is often drowned out by the noise of daily life. Meditation allows us to become still, to rest in the awareness of God's presence, and to listen for divine guidance.

Mindfulness, a related practice, encourages us to be fully present in each moment, observing our thoughts and emotions without judgment. This practice helps us develop a heightened awareness of how we react to external stimuli, allowing us to notice when we are acting from a place of fear, anxiety, or ego rather than from our authentic self. Through mindfulness, we begin to see the subtle ways in which we are often driven by unconscious patterns, and we can make conscious choices to respond differently.

In the practice of mindfulness, we recognize that self-discovery is not about achieving perfection but about becoming more aware of who we are in each moment. It is in this awareness that we can make choices aligned with our core values. For example, by practicing mindfulness in our daily interactions, we may notice when we are acting out of people-pleasing tendencies or when we are compromising our values to fit in. Once we recognize these patterns, we can begin to shift our behavior toward greater authenticity.

Spiritually, meditation and mindfulness help us align with God's will. As we quiet our minds, we open ourselves to the still, small voice of the Holy Spirit, guiding us toward greater understanding and alignment with our true purpose.

3. **Prayer and Scriptural Reflection:** Prayer is the

cornerstone of self-discovery. It is through prayer that we communicate with God, seeking His wisdom, guidance, and understanding. Prayer is not only about speaking to God but also about listening—listening for the ways in which God is revealing truths about ourselves. When we pray with the intention of self-discovery, we invite God into the process, asking Him to show us where we are out of alignment with His will and how we can live more fully in our purpose.

Scriptural reflection deepens this practice. The Bible is filled with wisdom about human nature, identity, and the journey of faith. Reflecting on scriptures that speak to our current struggles or desires helps us connect our personal growth with divine truth. For example, reflecting on Psalm 139:14, "I praise you because I am fearfully and wonderfully made," reminds us that our values and identity are rooted in God's creation, not in the expectations or judgments of others.

Regularly engaging with scripture allows us to see ourselves through God's eyes. It helps us remember that we are not defined by our past mistakes or present struggles but by our inherent worth as children of God.

4. **Spiritual Counseling or Therapy:** The journey of self-discovery often requires the guidance of a trusted counselor or therapist, especially when we are dealing with deep-seated wounds or unresolved trauma. A spiritual counselor or therapist can help us navigate the complexities of our inner world, offering insights that we may not be able to see on our own. Therapy provides a safe space to explore difficult emotions, examine past experiences, and work through patterns of behavior that are hindering our growth.

Spiritual counseling integrates psychological healing with spiritual growth. It helps us understand how our emotional wounds affect our spiritual life and vice versa. A counselor trained in both psychology and spirituality can guide us toward greater self-awareness and wholeness, helping us heal the parts of ourselves that have been fragmented by life's storms.

Therapy is not a sign of weakness but a courageous step toward healing and growth. It demonstrates a commitment to living authentically, with integrity and alignment.

5. **Body Awareness Practices:** Our bodies hold the memories of our emotional experiences. Practices like yoga, Tai Chi, or other body-centered disciplines help us release stored tension and become more attuned to the messages our bodies are sending us. These practices emphasize the integration of mind, body, and spirit, teaching us that true self-discovery involves listening not only to our thoughts and emotions but also to the wisdom of our physical bodies.

When we experience stress, fear, or unresolved emotions, our bodies respond with tension, discomfort, or illness. Body awareness practices help us reconnect with our bodies and release the stored energy that may be blocking our emotional or spiritual growth. For example, practicing yoga can help us release physical tension caused by emotional stress, allowing us to move through life with greater ease and alignment.

Body awareness also reminds us that we are whole beings—mind, body, and spirit. By caring for our physical health, we support our emotional and spiritual well-being.

One of the greatest obstacles to self-discovery is our reluctance to acknowledge our weaknesses. Society often pushes us to focus on strengths, success, and achievements, leaving little room for vulnerability. But true self-discovery involves embracing both our strengths and our weaknesses.

Recognizing our strengths allows us to live more fully and purposefully. Our strengths are gifts that enable us to contribute meaningfully to the world. Whether it is empathy, leadership, creativity, or perseverance, our strengths reflect the unique qualities God has bestowed upon us.

When we embrace our strengths, we gain confidence in our abilities. We stop trying to be what others want us to be and start living in alignment with our true selves. This alignment leads to a sense of fulfillment and joy, as we use our gifts for a higher purpose.

Conversely, acknowledging our weaknesses offers an opportunity for growth and humility. It reminds us that we are human, that we are not perfect, and that we do not have to be. Weaknesses are not flaws to be hidden but areas where we can invite God's grace to work in us.

In 2 Corinthians 12:9, Paul famously writes, "But He said to me, 'My grace is sufficient for you, for my power is made perfect in weakness.'" This scripture reminds us that our weaknesses are not obstacles to living a full life—they are opportunities for God's strength to shine through us.

When we accept our weaknesses, we stop striving for an unrealistic standard of perfection. Instead, we focus on growth, learning, and relying on God's grace. In doing so, we become more compassionate toward ourselves and others, recognizing that everyone has areas of struggle and growth.

Living authentically is the ultimate goal of self-discovery. It means that our actions, decisions, and behaviors align with our core values and beliefs. Authenticity is not about perfection; it is about integrity—being true to ourselves and our purpose.

To live authentically, we must first understand what matters most to us. Core values are the guiding principles that shape our decisions and actions. They are the non-negotiables in our lives—the things we stand for, no matter what.

Defining your core values requires introspection. Ask yourself: What do I believe in? What principles do I want to guide my life? For some, these values may be rooted in faith, family, honesty, or justice. For others, they may involve creativity, adventure, or service to others.

Once we have identified our core values, the next step is to align our actions with those beliefs. This can be challenging, especially when external pressures—such as societal expectations or the opinions of others—pull us in different directions.

Living authentically means making decisions that reflect our values, even when it is difficult. It may mean saying no to opportunities that do not align with our purpose, or it might involve standing up for what we believe in, even when it is unpopular.

Authenticity requires courage. It involves embracing

vulnerability and being willing to show the world who we truly are. In a culture that often celebrates conformity, living authentically can feel like swimming against the current. But it is in these moments of authenticity that we experience the deepest sense of peace and fulfillment.

When we fail to live authentically, we create dissonance within ourselves. This dissonance manifests as stress, anxiety, and a lack of fulfillment. We may find ourselves constantly seeking approval or validation from others, or we might feel disconnected from our purpose.

Living inauthentically can also lead to burnout. When our actions are misaligned with our values, we expend energy on things that do not truly matter to us. Over time, this takes a toll on our mental, emotional, and spiritual well-being.

By contrast, living in alignment with our values brings a sense of clarity and peace. We no longer waste energy trying to be someone we are not. Instead, we focus on living purposefully and meaningfully, guided by our true selves.

The journey of self-discovery is not a solo endeavor. As Psalm 23:2-4 reminds us, God is an ever-present guide, leading us beside still waters and restoring our souls. This restoration is crucial for knowing ourselves because it reconnects us with our divine source.

In the hustle and bustle of life, we rarely take time to be still. Yet, it is in these moments of stillness that we hear the voice of God and reconnect with our true selves. Stillness allows us to step away from the distractions and noise of the world, creating space for reflection and spiritual renewal.

In stillness, we come to understand that our worth is not determined by our accomplishments or failures. We are valuable simply because we are children of God. This realization is both freeing and empowering. It releases us from the pressure to prove ourselves and allows us to rest in the knowledge that we are already enough.

Self-discovery is not solely a human endeavor—it is deeply spiritual. As we explore our inner selves, we are invited to see ourselves through God's eyes. This perspective shifts our focus from worldly achievements to divine purpose. Instead of striving to be what society wants us to be, we begin to seek alignment with God's plan for our lives.

Psalm 23 speaks of restoration, reminding us that God heals the broken parts of our souls. Whether we have been wounded by life's storms or our own mistakes, God's grace is available to restore us. This restoration is not just a return to our previous state but a renewal that transforms us into the person God intended us to be.

Psalm 23 also speaks of walking in paths of righteousness for God's name's sake. This is a reminder that self-discovery is not just about understanding ourselves—it is about aligning our lives with God's purpose. Living authentically means walking in righteousness and making decisions that reflect our faith and values.

As we walk this path, we may encounter challenges and opposition. The world often pushes us to conform to its standards, but God calls us to a higher purpose. Walking in righteousness requires courage, conviction, and trust in

God's plan.

The journey of self-discovery is lifelong. It is not a destination to be reached but a process to be embraced. Along the way, there will be moments of clarity and moments of confusion, but each step brings us closer to understanding our true selves.

Remember, self-discovery is not about achieving perfection—it is about progress. It is about becoming more aware of who we are, what we believe, and how we want to live. And as we grow in self-awareness, we also grow in our capacity to love, serve, and fulfill our divine purpose.

Psalm 23 reminds us that we are not alone on this journey. God walks with us, leading us beside still waters, restoring our souls, and guiding us in paths of righteousness. As we continue to explore the "you, you need to know," may we find peace in the knowledge that we are fully known and fully loved by our Creator.

Chapter 9:

They Have a Story Too

Most of us pass through storms in life. They come uninvited at the most unexpected time, to test our potential for endurance, shake our faith, and disrupt our well-organized lives. They come in their own forms, loss, betrayal, illness, economic adversity-and are cruel reminders that life is essentially fragile. Though no two storms are alike, there is something common in them all that puts us together as humans.

Nature often reflects back to life some amazingly real parallels. Take the weather, for example: storms are created when particular conditions in the shifting pressures, humidity, and changes in temperature all combine. Some storms build in a gradual fashion, warning of their approach with gathering clouds and shifting winds. Others strike with sudden, unannounced ferocity. And so it is with life. Some trials announce themselves with subtle changes; others fall upon us with no hint of warning, catching us unprepared.

In such storms, it often feels very lonely outside, as if we were the only ones under fire. But since the rain will fall on both the just and the unjust, as indeed is the case with life's storms touching each and every human being, their presence reminds us that no man is an island in the grand scheme of existence. We are all capable of suffering.

And that's not a failing in the creation; that's an intrinsic feature within the design. Storms do test us, storms refine us, but above all, storms unite us. They strip away peripheral distinctions of wealth or status or education and reveal the common denominators of our humanness.

The Bible is full of storm stories, skies, and seas, metaphoric and real-lived by people to whom the purposes of God were made clear in allowing His people trials. Perhaps Job is the most famous of these, a man of great faith and a great builder of prosperity whose life was turned upside down by loss that was sure to devastate him. The story of Job speaks to profound suffering but also to the sovereignty of God: his trials served not only to refine his character but also to demonstrate the universality of human dependence on God.

Consider also the storm faced by the disciples in Mark 4:35-41. As they cross the Sea of Galilee, a sudden squall threatens to capsize their boat. Terrified, they awaken Jesus, crying out, "Teacher, don't you care if we drown?" Jesus calms the storm with a word but also uses the moment to question their faith: "Why are you so afraid? Do you still have no faith?

That's a powerful story to remind you that storms in your life are opportunities for your faith to grow. The fear in the hearts of the disciples was like yours and mine when we face trials and cry out to God, "Don't you care? Don't you see how much this hurts?" Yet again, the storm becomes the classroom, the place where God would show His power and teach deeper trust in Himself.

Even storms are not for nothing. While they often feel chaotic and unfair, the Word promises that God works all things together for good, even when we cannot see how.

Trials shape us in ways comfort cannot: they build perseverance, deepen empathy, and expose our dependence on God.

2 Corinthians 1:3-4: This is how Paul beautifully puts it in the record of the redemptive purpose of suffering:

Blessed be the God and Father of our Lord Jesus Christ, the Father of mercies and God of all comfort, who comforts us in all our affliction so that we may be able to comfort those who are in any affliction with the comfort with which we ourselves are comforted by God.

This passage reframes pain into preparation. It is in our trials that we are fitted to be vessels of God's comfort to others. And it is in these times of hardship that we are strengthened and given the tools to extend compassion to others on similar paths. Pain, then, is not only personal but communal. It links us to others in ways we might not have chosen but must learn to embrace.

This truth is manifested in people's stories. Take, for instance, a mother who lost her child. Her hurt is just about insurmountable, but over time, she learns to comfort others facing similar losses. Her storm, though devastating, becomes a healing balm to others. Or the addict who fought the addiction and emerged onto the other side, testimony to his journey became light for those still muddling in the darkness.

The storms we weather may not be solely about ourselves. They ripple outward, informing the lives of those with whom we connect. So, the pain becomes different when seen from its broader perspective. Our scars, painful as they are, may become some sort of map for others looking to find their way out of their own wilderness.

Recognizing the universality of storms, invites us into a posture of empathy. It exhorts us to dare to look beyond our pain at the pain of others. That does not always come quite so easily. When we are in the thick of our storms, it narrows our vision. The weight of our burdens may blur the capacity to notice the sufferings around us.

But the scripture calls us to bear one another's burdens. Galatians 6:2. This is not a command to act but an invitation to be transformed by such an act of connection. In someone else's story, our own pain shrinks. We are not alone; together, we are stronger.

Ultimately, we are in a position of comforting others because God comforts us. As Paul reminds us in 2 Corinthians, He is a "Father of compassion and the God of all comfort." God's comfort is anything but passive; it goes into action to meet us in our deepest pain and equips us with the same comfort to extend to others.

In our storms, just as we lean on God, we draw from a well that is infinite in grace. This grace allows us to stand the storms and empowers us to comfort others. In this process, trials turn into testimonies, and pains now become purposes.

And the storms will surely come-that's a given in life. Yet, within its universality does come the opportunity for connection, empathy, and divineness. Let us not forget-as we go about our own struggles-that others are enduring their storm. Their stories are just like ours: a big tapestry of resilience, faith, and grace.

Through God's comfort, we are called to be hands and feet to comfort and strengthen those around us. This chapter will consider how deeper faith, stronger communities, and living out our call to love one another all come through taking the time to understand other people's stories.

Storms are something absolutely inevitable in life, sometimes in various intensities and forms, but nobody is an exception. They put us in our places, focusing on our shared humanity, on the fragile yet resilient entity that we all are as human beings. Acknowledging the universality of life's trials can stir in our humility, empathy, and a deeper sense of connection with people around us.

Storms come for the rich executive, the farmer of that rural village, the widowed aged, and the teenager trying to find his place in the world. No amount of wealth, status, or knowledge can save us from their reach. A hurricane does not select its path based on the valuables it destroys in homes; metaphorical storms are not biased by any stretch.

This is a comforting and challenging universality. It reminds us that suffering is part of being human and not a sign of failure or heaven's punishment. Jesus, the Son of God, during His earthly ministry, was never a stranger to storms, literal and metaphorical. We find Him weeping at Lazarus's tomb; even the divine are not untouched by human pain.

Suffering is a shared reality, and the lessons it carries are found in the many different stories throughout the Bible, as individuals and communities make their way through storms.

1. The Widow of Zarephath (1 Kings 17:7-16):

Elijah finds the widow in preparation for the worst-a last meal for her and her son before they give in to the famine. Yet, it is a universal plight representative of the despair and helplessness storms usually bring with them. It is through her faith and obedience to Elijah's request that God made a miraculous provision of having her jar of flour and jug of oil never run out.

Two great truths are seen here: the fact that storms often bring us to a breaking point, and secondly, they set the stage for divine intervention. Similarly, the story of the widow represents that of so many who, quite literally, feel like they are on the edge yet still find hope in God's provision.

2. Paul's Thorn in the Flesh: 2 Corinthians 12:7-10

Paul is quite vulnerable in speaking of a continuing problem he refers to as "a thorn in the flesh." He begged God to take it away, but God replied, "My grace is sufficient for you, for my power is made perfect in weakness."

And all who undergo painful chronic pain, mental struggles, or trials that never seem to relent understand Paul's storm in a continuous struggle. It reminds us that storms are not getting over the way we might wish they end, as we may sometimes stay on with us for our good, to keep us near to God, and to purify faith.

The universality of storms is by no means unique to biblical accounts. History and literature are rich in such examples, as well as current events, when shared struggles come to unite and define communities.

1. Natural Disasters:

Argue the case of post-hurricanes, wildfires, or earthquakes: these catastrophes destroy whole communities yet bring them together in unbelievably incredible ways. Total strangers show camaraderie from neighborhood to neighborhood, and lines between "mine" and "yours" blur with the ++ idea that all are surviving together. Relief efforts, bravery tales, and acts of kindness during these events bring about the best of humanity amidst its vulnerability.

For example, immediately after the disaster brought on by Hurricane Katrina in the year 2005, tens of people and churches stood up and came forward to alleviate the problems of the displaced families. Though the storm brought great destruction, at the same time, it elicited acts of compassion and solidarity across socioeconomic and racial boundaries.

2. Global Health Crises:

The COVID-19 pandemic has underlined the interaction of human experience: fear, loss, isolation, and uncertainty that people are experiencing in all parts of the world. As much as the pandemic has underlined inequalities, it has equally shown the resilience of communities-from health workers who risk their lives for neighbours who deliver groceries to the vulnerable. The storm in pandemic juvenile humanity has brought to the fore the fragility and strength of humanity.

3. Economic Hardships:

Financial storms-coming in the form of job losses or recession-affect all manners of individuals and families. A formerly successful business owner and a single parent barely holding on join together, standing in lines at food banks. These mutual experiences of want and insecurity remind us that storms are great levelers; they eliminate differences and reinforce unity.

To realize that storms are everywhere is not a mute observation; it is a truth of perspective-changing caliber. It shifts our questions from "Why me?" to "Why not me?" and "How may I help others?"

That is a humble mentality. When we think that everybody is in some kind of storm, it closes the door to self-pity and entitlement. It reminds us that, in some sense, all people are connected and, together, can learn from each other and grow in the process.

Or let's say, for example, that a man loses his job and feels isolated and ashamed of it more often than not. As he tells his story to the rest, he realizes how many have faced similar challenges. Through these shared vulnerabilities, he gains not only practical advice but much-sought emotional support, as his storm is transformed into a bridge.

Once we acknowledge the universality of storms, we are summoned to respond in compassion. This starts by looking upon other people not as separate entities unto themselves but as companions on one's life journey.

It is so easy to judge people by the cover and genuinely think that they have no problems in life. Yet all of us carry our hidden crosses. The successful executive who is suffering from depression, the ever-smiling mother who is struggling to make both ends meet, and the confident teenager bogged down with anxiety disorders, all remind us that storms are not always seen.

As Paul writes in Galatians 6:2, "Carry each other's burdens, and in this way, you will fulfill the law of Christ." Empathy begins with the readiness to look beyond the surface and engage with the realities of others' lives.

Empathy doesn't need to imply taking on other people's problems; most of the time, it starts by being able to listen. When we take the time to listen to somebody's story, we acknowledge their humanness right there and create space for healing. Listening with compassion enables connection on deep levels and reminds others they are not alone.

Storms are universal, and they are not senseless. The storms strip us of all our illusions of being in control and being independent. All storms remind us how much we stand in need of God and people. In the recognition of the universality of suffering, we have opened ourselves to deeper connections, greater empathy, and a more significant meaning to life.

Every person has a story, which is like a reservoir of lessons. The story of others teaches us all about patience, faith, and the unyielding presence of God.

In the Bible, the story of Ruth offers profound lessons. A widow in a foreign land, Ruth's loyalty to her mother-in-law, Naomi, and her unwavering faith in God led to redemption and restoration. Her journey reminds us that even in unfamiliar and painful circumstances, faithfulness and humility can lead to unexpected blessings.

In our communities, testimonies of resilience are everywhere. A woman shares how she found peace amidst a devastating diagnosis, inspiring others to lean on their faith. A man recounts how forgiveness brought him freedom after years of estrangement from his father. These stories teach us to see God's hand in every situation, encouraging us to trust in His plan even when the path seems unclear.

Hearing these stories doesn't just inspire; it equips us. They remind us that storms, while challenging, are not insurmountable. Others have endured and triumphed, and so can we.

No one should face their storms alone. As members of a shared human experience, we are called to bear one another's burdens (Galatians 6:2). A supportive community is not just comforting; it is life-giving.

Building such a community begins with intentional acts of kindness and support. These actions may be as simple as offering a meal to a grieving neighbor or as profound as standing by a friend through a long season of trial. Small gestures—like a thoughtful text or a heartfelt prayer—can create ripples of hope.

Churches play a pivotal role in fostering these connections. They serve as sanctuaries where people can find solace and support. Small groups, prayer circles, and counseling ministries are all tools for building relationships that endure beyond Sunday services.

A truly supportive community reflects God's love. It's

a space where everyone feels seen, valued, and uplifted—a tangible reminder of His promise never to leave or forsake us.

Our ability to comfort others comes directly from the comfort we receive from God. As Paul writes in 2 Corinthians, our trials prepare us to be vessels of His compassion. This divine exchange is at the heart of the Christian faith: God meets us in our pain so that we can meet others in theirs.

Consider the story of the Good Samaritan (Luke 10:25-37). The Samaritan's willingness to help a stranger in distress exemplifies what it means to act as God's hands and feet. He didn't pass by the injured man; he stopped, tended to his wounds, and ensured his safety. His actions weren't just acts of kindness; they were reflections of God's love in action.

Prayer, too, plays a vital role in comforting others. When we intercede for someone, we invite God into their situation, trusting His power to bring healing and peace. Even when we feel powerless to help physically, prayer reminds us that God is always at work.

"They have a story too." These words challenge us to look beyond our own struggles and see the humanity in others. They call us to listen, to connect, and to extend the comfort we've received.

As we move forward, let us carry this truth with us: empathy and compassion are not just acts of kindness; they are acts of faith. They reflect the character of God and fulfill our calling as His children.

Lord, open our eyes to see the stories around us. Teach us to listen, to empathize, and to act as vessels of Your love. Help us to build communities that reflect Your grace and remind us that no one's storm is theirs to bear alone. Amen.

The story of Ruth in the Bible provides profound lessons. A widow in a foreign land, through faithfulness to her mother-in-law Naomi and God, entered a journey of redemption and restoration. Her personal journey reminds us that even through unfamiliar and painful circumstances, faithfulness and humility can bring forth unexpected blessings.

Stories of resilience are around us in our communities: a woman stood up and shared how, right in the middle of a devastating diagnosis, she found peace, encouraging others to lean on their faith. Others restart where they had left off, sharing how forgiving freed him after all those years he had lived estranged from his father. These testimonies are teaching us to see God's hand at work in everything that happens, trusting His plan despite the strategy not being clear.

These stories, when heard, don't just inspire us; they equip us. They remind us that though the storms may be hard, they are survivable. Others have gone through them, and made it to the other side, and we can, too.

No one must face his or her own storms alone. As brothers and sisters in that thing called life, we are called to bear one another's burdens. A supportive community is comforting, even life-giving.

That kind of community is built from intentional acts of

service and care. Such acts may be simple, like bringing a meal to a neighbor in sorrow, or profound, like standing alongside a friend through a hard, long season. Even small actions, a well-timed text or heart-felt prayer, can have ripples of hope.

Churches are very instrumental in offering these relationships. Churches are havens for most people to seek refuge when confronted with stressful situations. They also provide small groups, prayer circles, and sometimes counseling ministries to build a relationship that will last beyond Sunday morning services.

A supportive community is one that really reflects the love of God. It's where everybody is seen, valued, and uplifted; it's that reminder that God will never leave or forsake us.

For it is from the comfort we receive from God that our ability to comfort others originates. As Paul says in 2 Corinthians, it is through our own trials that we are fitted to become vessels for His compassion-so that He may be able to comfort others. This exchange is God's way and the core of the Christian faith: God meets us in our pain so that we can meet others in theirs.

The parable of the Good Samaritan is perhaps one example, in Luke 10:25-37, of what this means to be God's hands and feet in pragmatic ways. The Samaritan did not pass by the injured man; he stopped, tended his wounds, and made sure he was safe. In his actions, one sees reflected not acts of mere kindness but reflections of God's love in action.

But prayer also does a very important work in bringing

comfort to others. When we intercede for someone, we invite God into their situation-trusting. His power can heal and bring peace to the one who is hurting. It reminds us that even when we can do nothing physically to be of help, God is always at work.

They, too, have a story." These words challenge us to look beyond our own struggles and see the humanity in others; they call us to listen, to connect, and to extend the comfort we've received.

Now, let us take that truth with us into the days ahead: empathy and compassion-these are more than acts of kindness; they are acts of faith. They reflect the character of God and fulfill our calling as His children.

God, open our eyes to see around us so many stories. Teach us to listen, have empathy, and act as Your vessels of love. Help us create communities like Yours, filled with grace, reminding us no storm is ours alone to bear. Amen.

Chapter 10:

The Dissipating Stage

When the storm subsides, the immediate aftermath is often marked by a mixture of relief and weariness. The battle to survive may be over, but the journey of healing has just begun. In the dissipating stage, the focus shifts from enduring the storm to addressing the damage it left behind. Healing and recovery are not linear processes; they require patience, compassion, and intentional effort. This section explores the physical, emotional, and spiritual aspects of recovery, emphasizing that true healing must encompass the whole self.

Life's storms often exact a significant physical toll. Whether the storm was a prolonged period of stress or a single traumatic event, the body absorbs the impact. Symptoms of fatigue, tension, and even illness often emerge as the body processes the trauma. The first step toward healing is acknowledging this physical toll and allowing the body to rest and rejuvenate.

Rest is not a luxury but a necessity. Sleep, nutrition, and gentle movement are essential components of recovery. Rest gives the body a chance to repair itself, to recover from the high levels of adrenaline and cortisol that storms often trigger. In moments of rest, the mind begins to clear, and the path to emotional and spiritual recovery becomes visible.

The emotional aftermath of a storm is often complex and layered. Relief may mingle with grief, and hope may be shadowed by residual fear. These emotions can arise unexpectedly, like waves that follow an initial surge. Allowing oneself to feel these emotions is crucial. Suppressing or denying them only prolongs the healing process.

Journaling is one effective tool for navigating this emotional landscape. Writing allows for the safe exploration of feelings, thoughts, and fears. It creates a private space to process the storm's impact and articulate what words may struggle to express in conversations. Likewise, therapy or counseling can provide invaluable guidance, offering tools to understand and cope with lingering emotional wounds.

Isaiah 43:2 reminds us of God's promise to be with us through the most challenging times: "When you go through deep waters, I will be with you." The dissipating stage is a profound opportunity for spiritual renewal. Storms often leave us feeling disconnected from our inner selves and the divine, but they also offer the chance to rebuild a deeper connection.

Prayer and meditation provide solace, creating moments of stillness where divine guidance can be felt. Reflecting on scripture helps anchor the soul, reminding us that storms do not have the power to define us. Instead, they refine us. This spiritual practice is not about seeking immediate answers but about cultivating trust in the process of healing.

Healing is rarely a solitary journey. While solitude offers space for self-reflection, community provides the support necessary for recovery. Whether through family, friends, or faith-based groups, leaning on others fosters resilience. Their encouragement can rekindle hope, while their presence reminds us that we are not alone in our struggles.

Reaching out can feel daunting, especially if the storm involves relational conflict or isolation. However, vulnerability is often met with compassion and understanding. Healing conversations and shared experiences create bonds that carry us forward.

Healing requires self-compassion, an often-overlooked aspect of recovery. Self-compassion involves treating oneself with the same kindness and understanding that we would offer a dear friend. It means releasing the guilt, shame, or self-criticism that storms can generate.

Mantras or affirmations can reinforce self-compassion. Phrases like "I am worthy of healing" or "This pain is temporary" provide encouragement in moments of doubt. Gradually, these affirmations reframe the narrative of the storm, transforming it from a story of suffering to one of resilience and growth.

Just as a storm leaves physical debris in its wake, life storms leave emotional and spiritual clutter that must be cleared. This process involves identifying and releasing what no longer serves us. Letting go of bitterness, regret, or unrealistic expectations clears space for new growth.

Metaphorically, this stage is like tending a garden after a storm. We remove broken branches and uproot weeds, making way for fresh blooms. The effort is painstaking but necessary, and the result is a restored, flourishing inner world.

The first glimmers of hope often appear in the healing stage. Hope does not demand that we have all the answers or that the path ahead is clear. Instead, it invites us to trust that healing is possible and that better days lie ahead. By nurturing hope, we anchor ourselves to a vision of wholeness and peace.

The emotional and spiritual journey of recovery is profound and deeply personal. Healing is not about returning to who we were before the storm but about becoming someone stronger, wiser, and more compassionate. By prioritizing rest, emotional exploration, spiritual renewal, and community support, we lay the foundation for a brighter future. The dissipating stage is not the end; it is the beginning of a renewed, empowered self.

The aftermath of a storm often reveals the stark reality of what has been lost. Destruction may be physical, emotional, or spiritual, and in this clarity, the enormity of the work ahead can feel overwhelming. Yet, within this rubble lies a quiet but profound invitation: the chance to rebuild not just what was broken but to create something stronger, more enduring, and more aligned with who you are becoming.

Rebuilding begins with the delicate process of surveying the damage. This is not merely a mechanical assessment of what has been lost, but a deeply personal journey through memories, emotions, and lessons. Just as one would walk through a storm-ravaged home, identifying what can be salvaged and what must be let go, we must take stock of our inner and outer worlds. There is a certain courage required in this act—to look directly at the brokenness, to acknowledge the losses, and to accept that some pieces may never be the same. But with this courage comes an opportunity to reshape the future, rooted in the wisdom gained from what has been endured.

In the quiet of this stage, you might find yourself revisiting relationships, dreams, and aspects of life that were once taken for granted. Storms have a way of exposing what is fragile or neglected, forcing us to confront truths we might otherwise avoid. A friendship that withered under strain, a career that felt hollow even before the chaos, or a spiritual life that seemed distant—all of these become clearer in the stillness. Rebuilding is not about restoring everything to its former state; it is about sifting through the debris to discern what is worth preserving and what must be left behind. This process is deeply personal and, at times, painful, but it is also transformative.

True rebuilding is an act of transformation. It asks us not only to patch up what is broken but to imagine what could be. It requires creativity, resilience, and the willingness to envision a life that may look different from the one before the storm. Consider a house rebuilt after a hurricane—often, it is constructed with stronger materials and thoughtful design, intended to withstand future challenges. In the same way, the process of rebuilding your life calls for intentionality and foresight.

The first steps might feel small and tentative, like planting seeds in uncertain soil. Perhaps it begins with setting new routines, reaching out to repair a strained relationship, or reconnecting with a dream long left dormant. Each of these acts, however minor they may seem, contributes to the foundation of what is to come. At times, it may feel like progress is slow, and the temptation to revert to old patterns might arise. But rebuilding is not about speed; it is about depth and integrity.

Rebuilding is rarely a solitary endeavor, though the initial impulse might be to retreat inward, to shoulder the weight alone. There is vulnerability in asking for help, in admitting that you cannot do it all on your own. Yet, this vulnerability is where strength begins. In the aftermath of a storm, communities often come together to rebuild not just physical structures but the bonds that sustain them. The same holds true in personal rebuilding.

Leaning on others—whether family, friends, or a spiritual community—creates a network of support that makes the work lighter. These connections remind us that we are not alone, even when the path ahead feels daunting. There is power in shared stories, in hearing how others have weathered their own storms and found ways to rebuild. Their resilience becomes a source of inspiration, and their presence offers comfort in moments of doubt.

Spiritual communities, in particular, often play a unique role in this phase. They provide not only practical support but also a shared sense of purpose and hope. Whether through shared prayer, collective acts of service, or simply the act of being present, these communities embody the idea that we are stronger together. The humility to accept help fosters deeper connections, and in those connections, healing and rebuilding intertwine.

As the work progresses, a shift occurs. What once felt like rubble begins to take shape, and the vision of a new foundation emerges. This is a pivotal moment in the dissipating stage—a time to ensure that what you are building is not merely a reflection of what once was but a testament to what you have learned.

Storms often reveal weaknesses that were previously hidden. Perhaps the storm exposed a lack of boundaries in a relationship, a financial instability that left you vulnerable, or an overreliance on external validation. These revelations, though difficult to confront, are gifts in disguise. They offer the chance to address underlying issues and create a stronger, more stable foundation.

This process is not without its challenges. Rebuilding often requires letting go of old patterns, beliefs, or even relationships that no longer serve you. There may be moments of resistance, where the familiar feels safer than the unknown. But it is in these moments that growth happens. Each decision to build with intention—to prioritize health, stability, and purpose—is a step toward a future that is not just rebuilt but reimagined.

Throughout the process, faith becomes both a guide and a source of strength. Rebuilding is an act of hope, and hope is deeply intertwined with faith. Isaiah 43:2 reminds us of God's unwavering presence, a promise that sustains us when the work feels too heavy. Prayer, scripture, and moments of quiet reflection serve as anchors, grounding us in the knowledge that we are not rebuilding alone.

Faith also reminds us that progress is often invisible at first. Like seeds taking root beneath the soil, the fruits of our labor may not be immediately apparent. This requires perseverance—the willingness to continue building even when the results feel distant. It is in this perseverance that resilience is forged, and over time, the once-devastated landscape begins to bloom.

Rebuilding is not merely an act of restoration; it is a process of renewal. It is a chance to create a life that reflects the strength, wisdom, and clarity gained from the storm. Each brick laid, each decision made with intention, contributes to a life that is both resilient and meaningful.

In the end, the rubble becomes a foundation. What once seemed like destruction transforms into the starting point for something new. The process of rebuilding teaches us that while storms may break us, they do not define us. It is what we do after the storm—how we choose to heal, grow, and rebuild—that shapes who we are.

The work is not easy, but it is sacred. Every step, no matter how small, is a testament to the human spirit's ability to endure and to create. And in that creation, there is not just recovery but renewal—a renewal that carries within it the seeds of hope, strength, and a future that is brighter than we could have imagined.

The dissipating stage is not merely a time to heal and rebuild but also a season of profound learning. Every storm leaves its mark, not just in what it takes away but in what it teaches. In the aftermath, when the immediate chaos has subsided, a unique opportunity emerges—the chance to extract wisdom from the experience and use it to prepare for whatever may come next. Life's storms are inevitable, but the way we face them can transform, shaped by the lessons of the past.

The first step in preparing for future storms is reflection. In the stillness after the storm, the mind naturally revisits what happened: the choices made, the challenges faced, and the outcomes that unfolded. At first, this reflection may feel like reliving the storm, but over time, it becomes a pathway to insight.

Reflection allows us to see the storm from a distance, no longer swept up in its immediate demands. We begin to notice patterns—perhaps moments when we ignored early warning signs or areas where we lacked the resources to cope effectively. These realizations are not meant to foster regret but to illuminate opportunities for growth. What did the storm reveal about your strengths? Where did it expose vulnerabilities? These questions guide the process of preparing for the future.

Importantly, reflection is not a solitary exercise. Sharing your story with trusted confidants can bring fresh perspectives. Sometimes, others see strengths and lessons we overlook in ourselves. A friend might point out the courage you showed, while a spiritual mentor might help you discern how God was present even in moments of despair. These conversations deepen understanding and transform reflection into wisdom.

As the lessons of the storm come into focus, the next step is to cultivate awareness. Life often provides subtle warnings before a storm strikes, but they can be easy to miss in the rush of daily life. By staying attuned to these signals, we empower ourselves to act proactively rather than reactively.

This heightened awareness might manifest as a deeper sensitivity to relational dynamics, noticing when tensions begin to simmer rather than waiting for a conflict to erupt. Or it could take the form of financial vigilance, recognizing unsustainable spending patterns before they escalate into a crisis. In all areas of life, awareness becomes a tool for resilience, enabling us to face challenges with clarity and confidence.

Resilience, however, is not merely about anticipating storms. It is also about fortifying the foundations of your life so that when storms inevitably come, they cannot shake you as easily. This might mean strengthening emotional resilience through practices like mindfulness and gratitude, or cultivating spiritual resilience by deepening your relationship with God. The tools you develop during this stage become anchors, grounding you when new challenges arise.

The spiritual dimension of preparation cannot be overstated. Storms often shake us to our core, challenging not only our circumstances but our sense of purpose and connection. In the dissipating stage, as you reflect on the role of faith in your journey, you may find new ways to deepen that connection and prepare your spirit for future trials.

Faith acts as both a shield and a guide. It reminds us that we are never alone, even in the darkest moments, and it offers a framework for making sense of suffering. As you prepare for future storms, consider how spiritual practices can become a regular part of your life, not just a refuge during times of crisis. Prayer, scripture, and worship are not merely acts of devotion; they are tools that strengthen the soul.

Isaiah 43:2 serves as a powerful reminder of this truth: *"When you go through deep waters, I will be with you."* The promise of divine presence is a source of unshakable hope. By anchoring yourself in this promise, you cultivate a faith that endures, regardless of what storms may come.

Spiritual preparation also involves building a community of faith. Surrounding yourself with people who share your beliefs creates a support network that can sustain you in difficult times. These individuals become companions in both prayer and action, offering wisdom, encouragement, and practical help when needed.

While spiritual readiness provides the foundation, practical measures are also essential. The lessons of the storm often point to specific areas where preparation is needed. Perhaps the storm revealed a lack of financial security, prompting you to create an emergency savings fund. Or maybe it highlighted the importance of maintaining open communication with loved ones, leading to intentional efforts to strengthen those relationships.

Preparation looks different for everyone, but some common strategies include:

- **Financial Stability**: Building savings, reducing debt, and creating a budget provide a cushion against unexpected challenges.

- **Relational Investment**: Taking the time to nurture

meaningful connections ensures that your support system remains strong.

- **Health and Wellness**: Prioritizing physical and mental health creates a foundation of strength and resilience.

Preparation is not about living in fear of the future. Rather, it is an act of empowerment, a way to face life's uncertainties with confidence. When the next storm arrives, you will not be starting from scratch. Instead, you will draw on the tools, lessons, and resources cultivated during this time, meeting the challenge with clarity and courage.

As you prepare, it is important to strike a balance between vigilance and trust. Vigilance involves staying attuned to potential challenges and taking proactive steps to address them. Trust, on the other hand, acknowledges that not every storm can be predicted or prevented. It is the recognition that control has its limits and that, ultimately, we must rely on faith and resilience to carry us through.

This balance is beautifully illustrated in the metaphor of a lighthouse. A lighthouse does not stop storms from occurring, nor can it guide every ship to safety. Its purpose is to provide a steady light, a point of reference that helps sailors navigate the chaos. In the same way, preparation does not eliminate life's storms, but it offers a sense of direction and stability in their midst.

Trusting in God's guidance is an integral part of this balance. It allows us to release the anxiety of trying to control every outcome and instead focus on what we can do, knowing that grace will fill the gaps. This trust is not passive; it is an active choice to lean into faith, even when the path ahead is uncertain.

One of the greatest gifts of preparing for future storms is the perspective it brings. Having survived a storm, you carry a deeper understanding of your own resilience and the strength of your faith. This perspective changes the way you approach challenges, replacing fear with confidence and uncertainty with hope.

You begin to see storms not as threats but as opportunities for growth. While they may disrupt and challenge, they also refine and transform. This shift in perspective does not diminish the difficulty of storms, but it reframes their purpose. They are no longer simply events to endure; they become chapters in a larger story of grace and growth.

Preparing for future storms is an act of wisdom born from experience. It is a process of reflection, growth, and intentionality, rooted in the knowledge that while storms may be inevitable, their impact is not. By cultivating awareness, strengthening faith, and taking practical steps, you equip yourself to face life's challenges with courage and hope.

As the promise of Isaiah 43:2 reminds us, the waters may rise, but they will not overwhelm us. With this assurance, we can approach the future not with fear but with confidence, knowing that we are prepared to weather whatever comes our way.

When the storm has passed, and the work of healing and rebuilding is well underway, a quieter season emerges—a time of peace and stability. This is not simply the absence of chaos; it is the presence of something deeper. Peace after a storm is a hard-won gift, one that comes from persevering through challenges and discovering resilience. Stability, meanwhile, is the foundation that allows this peace to endure. Together, they create a space to rest, reflect, and thrive.

The dissipating stage culminates in this sacred time. It is a moment to savor the life that remains, to celebrate the growth that has occurred, and to find joy in the simplicity of being. Embracing peace and stability is both an act of gratitude and an acknowledgment that life is not defined by storms but by how we live between and beyond them.

Peace after a storm is not always immediate. At first, the absence of turmoil may feel strange or even unsettling. Survivors often speak of a phenomenon known as "calm unease," where the quiet feels temporary, as though the storm might return at any moment. This is a natural response, born of the heightened vigilance that survival requires. Over time, however, this unease gives way to a more enduring sense of calm—a recognition that the storm has truly passed and that it is safe to let go.

The peace that follows a storm is unique because it carries the weight of experience. It is not a naïve peace, untested by hardship, but a mature peace that understands the value of stillness. This peace is rooted in the knowledge that while storms may come, they are not permanent. It is a peace that allows you to exhale deeply, to release tension that has been carried for far too long, and to embrace the present moment with open arms.

Stability, like peace, does not arise overnight. It is the product of the intentional work done during the rebuilding process. A stable life is one that feels anchored, where the foundations are secure, and where the fear of collapse no longer overshadows every decision. Stability does not mean that life is free of challenges, but it does mean that you have the tools and support to navigate them without being uprooted.

This stability is often multidimensional, encompassing emotional, spiritual, and practical aspects of life. Emotionally, stability means finding balance—a state where you are not constantly reacting to external circumstances but instead responding with clarity and purpose. Spiritually, stability is a deep-rooted faith that remains steady even in uncertainty. Practically, it involves having systems and routines that provide structure and reliability. Together, these dimensions create a life that feels whole and grounded.

Gratitude is one of the most powerful forces in the dissipating stage. It transforms the experience of survival into something more profound—a celebration of life and its resilience. Gratitude shifts focus from what was lost to what remains, from the pain of the storm to the strength it revealed.

For many, practicing gratitude becomes a daily ritual. It might take the form of writing in a gratitude journal, where even the smallest blessings are acknowledged and cherished. Others find gratitude in prayer, offering thanks to God for His presence and provision throughout the storm. Acts of kindness, such as helping others who are still in the midst of their own storms, also become expressions of gratitude, extending the grace you have received.

Gratitude is not about denying the difficulties of the storm. Instead, it is about holding those difficulties alongside the beauty that emerged from them. It is about recognizing that even in moments of hardship, there were glimmers of hope, acts of kindness, and lessons learned. By embracing gratitude, you transform survival into thriving, creating a life that feels abundant and full.

The dissipating stage offers a profound invitation: to live fully in the present. After the chaos and uncertainty of the storm, the present moment becomes a refuge—a place where you can find joy, simplicity, and contentment.

Living in the present requires letting go of two opposing tendencies: dwelling on the past and fearing the future. The past, with its wounds and regrets, can feel like a heavyweight, pulling you backward. The future, with its unknowns, can provoke anxiety, making it difficult to enjoy the here and now. Embracing the present means releasing both, allowing yourself to fully inhabit the moment at hand.

In practical terms, this might mean savoring small pleasures—a quiet morning with a cup of tea, a walk in nature, or a meaningful conversation with a loved one. These moments, though simple, become profound when experienced with intention. They remind us that life is not only about grand milestones but also about the beauty found in everyday moments.

Stillness is perhaps the most sacred gift of the dissipating stage. It is a space where the soul can rest, where the noise of the storm is replaced by a profound quiet. In this stillness, there is an opportunity to connect deeply—with yourself, with others, and with God.

Stillness allows for reflection, not just on the storm but on the journey of life as a whole. It is a time to consider where you have been, where you are now, and where you hope to go. This reflection is not rushed or pressured; it unfolds naturally, guided by the rhythm of peace.

For those who are spiritually inclined, stillness often becomes a space for communion with God. It is in these quiet moments that His presence feels most tangible, a reminder of the promise in Isaiah 43:2: *"When you go through deep waters, I will be with you."* In the stillness, you may find not only peace but also a renewed sense of purpose—a calling to live fully and to share the wisdom gained from your journey.

The peace and stability of the dissipating stage are not an end but a beginning. They provide the foundation for a life that is not just about surviving but about flourishing. This life is marked by resilience, gratitude, and a deep appreciation for the present. It is a life that carries the lessons of the storm without being defined by them—a life that embraces both its challenges and its joys.

As you move forward, you may find that storms no longer hold the same power over you. Where once they provoked fear, they now evoke a quiet confidence. You have faced the winds and the waves, and you have emerged stronger. This strength, coupled with the peace and stability you have cultivated, becomes a source of inspiration for others. Your story, shaped by the storm, becomes a testament to the power of faith, resilience, and renewal.

The dissipating stage concludes not with fanfare but with a deep sense of contentment. It is the beauty of calm waters after a tempest, the stillness that speaks of both survival and transformation. In this stage, you come to see the storm not as a chapter of destruction but as a chapter of growth.

Peace and stability are gifts that come from perseverance. They remind us that while storms may rage, they are not the final word. Beyond the storm lies a life of hope, renewal, and joy—a life grounded in the unshakable truth that we are never alone, that we are always growing, and that even the darkest clouds carry the seeds of light.

The dissipating stage is more than an ending—it is a beginning. Through healing, rebuilding, and preparation, we emerge stronger, wiser, and more resilient. Isaiah 43:2 reminds us that we are never alone; God walks with us through every stage, guiding us toward renewal.

In embracing this sacred time, we find that storms, though challenging, are not merely disruptions. They are opportunities for transformation, revealing the strength, wisdom, and peace that resides within us.